CHAPTER 1

This part of Paris hadn't changed much since the Revolution. Faceless tenements brooded on either side of the street. A thin stream of dirty water ran along a channel worn into the middle of the ancient lane. The leather soles of Nick Carter's shoes made a flat, hard sound on cobblestones that had echoed with the rumble of carts ferrying victims to the guillotine. Selena Connor walked beside him.

Selena wore a casual outfit she'd picked up in one of the designer salons. Designers loved making clothes for women like her. She was the kind of woman people noticed, with the elegance and body to carry it off. Sunglasses hid her violet eyes. Her reddish-blonde hair and tall, athletic grace turned heads wherever they went.

Nick had on a gray sport coat Selena had seen in one of the shop windows. It was always hard to find something that handled his broad shoulders but this one had fit perfectly, right off the rack. *It matches your eyes*, she'd said. His eyes were gray, flecked with gold, so it was close enough. He'd bought it to please her, because she liked it. Secretly, it pleased him, too. The European styling of the jacket and a half-day's black stubble on his chin almost made him look like a local.

They came to a shop window where a leather-bound edition of Voltaire's collected works was displayed on a bed of faded red cloth.

"This is it," she said.

The shop looked like it might have been new when Marie Antoinette was telling people to eat cake. It had a wooden door painted blue and old iron hinges. There was a sign in gold leaf written on the dusty glass of the window.

Jean-Paul Bertrand, le Propriétaire

Livres Rares et Curieux

Selena reached for the bell pull and stopped.

"That's odd," she said.

"What's odd?"

"The door is open," she said. "That's not right."

It was, by about two inches.

"Jean-Paul said to ring and he'd let us in. He keeps the door locked. You can only get in by appointment."

She pushed the door open the rest of the way and they entered the shop.

"Jean-Paul?" Selena called.

Her voice was clear, vibrant. There was no response.

The front room of the shop was deserted. Shelves filled with books lined two of the walls. An antique oak reading table with carved feet took up space in the front, near the window. The place smelled of old books, of dust and paper. In the back of the room was a zinc counter. Behind it, a beaded glass curtain hung in front of a passage leading to the rear of the shop.

"Jean-Paul?" Selena called again. "Hello? It's Selena."

Nick's ear itched. "Something's not right," he said. He tugged at his scarred ear. Without thinking, he reached for his gun. It wasn't there. They were on vacation. No guns.

"He's an old man," she said, "and he doesn't hear well. He's probably in the back."

Selena stepped around the counter and parted the beads. The hall was narrow and dark and close. There was a light at the end. She walked down the hall and pushed aside another curtain. Nick bumped into her as Selena stopped short.

Selena's friend lay on his back on the floor, mouth gaping. His teeth were yellow from years of nicotine and coffee. His eyes were open, staring at the ceiling. Blood covered his white shirt and spattered the walls. Books and papers littered the floor. The room stank of death.

9

"Jean-Paul," Selena said. Her face was white. She started toward him.

Nick stopped her with a hand on her shoulder. "Better not touch him." He went to the body.

"Look at this."

She came over and looked down at the floor. Letters and a number were written there in blood.

"Does it make any sense to you?" Nick asked.

EX 25

"No. Who would do this? I don't think he had an enemy in the world."

"He had at least one."

Nick gestured at the mess. The room had been searched by someone who didn't care about cleaning up afterward.

"Whoever killed him was looking for something."

"He had some valuable first editions. It must have been a robbery."

"This is over the top for a lousy book, even one worth a lot of money. An old man like this, they didn't need to kill him. Makes me angry."

"He sounded stressed when I talked with him. He was insistent that I come see him today."

"You didn't tell me that."

She looked at the body of her friend. "I didn't think anything of it." She bit her lip.

"I'm sorry, Selena."

"What now?"

"We call the cops. Then I'm going to call Harker. I don't want to spend the night in a French jail."

Director Elizabeth Harker was their boss. She ran the Project and had the clout to get the French cops to back off. The President's authority went a long way.

Four hours later, the police let them go back to their hotel. They were staying in the Le Marais District, on the Right

Bank, in the kind of European hostelry where you left your key at the desk when you went out and the desk clerk was always courteous. It was a friendly place. It didn't hurt any that Selena spoke French like a native.

"*Bon jour, Madame,*" the clerk said. "Something came for you."

He took a package from under the counter. It was wrapped in plain brown paper and addressed to Selena. There was no return address.

"By messenger. It arrived this afternoon, while you were out." He handed it to her with the room key.

"*Merci.*"

She looked at the address on the package. "This is from Jean-Paul," she said to Nick. "I recognize his writing."

The hotel had an ancient cage elevator. They clanked at a snail's pace to their floor.

Their room was large and looked out over a narrow balcony onto a quiet street. There was a private bath, a dresser and television, a wide bed covered with a patterned comforter and two comfortable armchairs. Nick sank into one of the chairs. Selena came out of the bathroom and sat on the bed.

"I wonder what this is?"

"Why not open it and find out?"

"Smartass." She gave him a look and tore off the wrapping.

"It's a file."

She took out a file folder tied with a length of red string and undid the tie. Inside the folder was a manuscript, yellowed and brittle, written in a cramped hand in black ink.

Selena looked at the first page. Nick heard her take in a deep breath.

"I don't believe this." There was excitement in her voice. "This was written by Nostradamus. I think these might be the lost quatrains."

"Nostradamus? The prophet?"

"Yes."

"What are the lost quatrains?"

"Nostradamus published his prophecies in groups of one hundred, called centuries. Each prophecy had four lines."

"A quatrain."

She nodded. "The Seventh Century is incomplete. There are 58 quatrains missing. No one has ever seen them. This manuscript is beyond rare."

"Rare enough to kill for?"

"Oh, yes. There are collectors who would give anything for this. Not only that, I think the writing is by Nostradamus himself. A hand written manuscript by Nostradamus would be worth a lot. The lost quatrains in his own hand would be priceless."

"This is probably what Bertrand's killer was looking for," Nick said. "Why send it to you?"

"I've known him since I was a child. He and my uncle were old friends."

"Maybe he meant it as a gift."

"No. If it were a gift he would have given it to me in person. He must have wanted to get it out of the shop." She paused. "Whoever murdered him could come looking for it. If they know he sent it to me."

"We should take it to the Embassy and send it home in a diplomatic pouch. "

"You want to keep it?"

"You want to find out who killed your friend? There's a reason he sent this to you. We won't know what it is unless you read it."

"No one just reads Nostradamus. He was worried about the Inquisition. He played word games and wrote in Greek and Latin and Provencal. Everything is deliberately obscure."

"Can you do it?"

Selena was a world class authority when it came to translating difficult texts and languages.

"Probably. But if we keep it, we're holding back evidence."

"If we don't keep it, the French police will keep us. Cops are suspicious. They'll think we killed him to get our hands on this."

Selena looked out the window. "You're right. Let's go to the Embassy."

She put the manuscript back in the file and the file back in the box. She tucked the box under her arm. They went downstairs and handed in the key and left the hotel. They started down the street to find a cab.

Movement in an alley on the right. A man came at them, knife held low, the blade gleaming in the afternoon light. Nick parried with his arm, the move born of years of practice and training. The blade sliced through the new jacket, into his arm. He followed through with an elbow strike to the skull that numbed his arm. He stiffened the fingers on his other hand and drove them like a spear up into the man's diaphragm, trying to rupture it. The attacker doubled over and Nick brought both hands down and drove a knee into his face. The man went down, blood pouring from his nose. The knife clattered away on the sidewalk.

A second man went for the package under Selena's arm. She let it go, twisted and kicked out from the hip and landed on the side of his chest with her foot. His ribs made a dull crunching sound. He screamed in pain and fell to the ground. She kicked him in the head. He stopped screaming.

Nick rubbed his elbow and looked down at them. One man was unconscious, the other moaned and writhed on the sidewalk. The whole fight had taken less than twenty seconds. Across the way, an elderly couple stared at them.

Selena's face was tight. She was breathing hard, her breath pushing out between half open lips. She looked at his arm.

"You're bleeding," she said.

Dark blood oozed through the rip in his sleeve.

"It's just a scratch."

Selena bent down and picked up the box with the Nostradamus file. Nick looked up and down the street. A crowd was beginning to gather.

"We need to get out of here," he said, "before the cops show up."

"Some vacation," she said.

CHAPTER TWO

The new Project headquarters sat on eighty acres of prime
countryside in the County of Fairfax, Virginia, within easy
commuting distance of the Capitol.

A twelve foot chain link fence all around the property
served to keep animals and the curious away. The real security
was automated and invisible. The main building looked like a
private home. It was vaguely colonial in style, with a columned
front porch, white siding and a sloping green shingle roof.
False wooden shutters painted green accented the windows.

A wide, paved driveway ran from the entry gate and guard
station to the house. Across from the house was a low concrete
building with overhead doors. It was empty, a space waiting for
a purpose. The drive ended in a cement helipad marked with a
wide, yellow circle. Washington and the White House were
minutes away by helicopter.

During the Cold War the property had been a Nike missile
site, with three 5000 square foot underground magazines of
hardened concrete and steel. Two of the magazines had been
covered over and landscaped, the only clue to their existence a
series of low ventilation pipes rising from the garden and lawn.
The house sat over the third.

The previous owner had converted the magazine directly
below the house into an emergency second home. It came with
a kitchen, bath, bedrooms, swimming pool and independent
power supply. The living area served as an operations center. A
second magazine housed the Project's Cray computers and
communication gear. The third contained a workout room, an
armory, and a pistol range. Access to the lower levels was from
inside the house, down a spiral staircase. A tool shed in the
flower garden outside concealed an emergency exit from
below.

Selena and Nick had come straight from the airport. Selena was behind the wheel of her burgundy-colored Mercedes. Nick eyed the house as they drove in. After the old headquarters had been destroyed, Harker had found a more secure location.

"I'm still not used to this," he said. "When Harker said we needed to go underground, I didn't think she meant it literally."

"You have to admit it's great camouflage. Lamont really likes the pool. So do I." Lamont Cameron was part of the team, recruited after he'd left the Navy Seals.

She parked in front of the house. They went up the steps onto the porch. A camera over the entrance tracked them. There was a biometric reader and facial recognition scanner by the door. Selena placed her thumb against the reader and leaned in to the scanner. The door opened with an oiled whisper of retracting bolts.

Director Elizabeth Harker's new office was in the back, on the ground floor. Elizabeth was at her desk, facing out through a wall of French windows onto a wide flower garden. The windows looked like regular windows, but even a fifty caliber round would have trouble getting through them. Elizabeth had decided the risk was worth it. In the old building, she'd been without a window for years.

Harker was a small woman. She was dressed in her usual outfit of black suit and crisp white blouse. She had milk white skin and emerald earrings that picked up the color of her eyes. Her hair was deep black with streaks of gray and white. There was a dimpled scar above her left eye, where an assassin's bullet had failed to kill her.

Nick thought she was the most competent woman he'd ever known. Her looks and small size deceived people who didn't know her into thinking she could be manipulated. It didn't take long for them to find out they were mistaken. Elizabeth Harker was nobody's pawn.

A large, flat screen monitor took up most of one wall in the office. A leather couch and three chairs were arranged near the desk. On Harker's desktop were the Nostradamus file, a pen and pad, and a picture of her father in a silver frame. The picture had replaced a photograph of the Twin Towers on 911, lost with everything else on the day the old headquarters was destroyed.

Elizabeth drew strength from the picture of her father. He'd had a practical way of getting to the heart of any problem with a quote or a quiet conversation. The Judge had died years before, but she still thought of his advice at times when she needed to make a critical decision.

She looked up as Nick and Selena came in. "The French are unhappy," she said. Harker never wasted words

They sat down on the couch.

"Hello to you too," Nick said. "What's their problem?"

"You mean aside from the fact that you put two of their nationals in a hospital and disappeared?"

"I thought it was best if we got out of the country."

"Fortunately for you, the two who attacked you were on Interpol's wanted list. What got the French upset was finding out Bertrand sent a package to your hotel the afternoon he was killed. They want to know what it was."

Elizabeth picked up her new pen. Her silver pen had been lost with everything else in the old office. She'd replaced it with a Mont Blanc, black with the trademark snowcap on the end. She began tapping it on the hard wooden surface of the desk.

"It seems that Selena's friend had some questionable contacts."

"What kind of contacts?" Selena asked.

"There's an underground black market trade in Europe for rare books. Interpol was keeping an eye on Bertrand."

"I don't believe Jean-Paul was dealing in the black market," Selena said. "He was an honest man. His books had provenance. All his contacts were legitimate."

"Not all of them. The police looked through his phone records. He got a call from someone connected to the Union Corse the morning of the day he was killed."

"What's the Union Corse?" Nick asked.

"The French Mafia. They're based in Corsica and Marseille. Big in the narcotics trade, art theft, prostitution, money laundering. The men who went after you were gangsters, members of the mob. It can't be a coincidence."

"You think the Union Corse killed Jean-Paul?"

"Yes. I told the French I'd talk to you. I didn't tell them we had this." She tapped the Nostradamus file with her finger. "Have you figured out what Bertrand meant by what he wrote on the floor?"

Selena brushed a hair from her forehead with the back of her hand. "No. It makes no sense to me."

Harker pushed the file folder across the desk. "I want you to translate this. We might learn something."

"I can translate it, but I can't guarantee I'll understand it. Not with Nostradamus."

"Work with Stephanie. Use the computers to speed things up."

Stephanie Willits was Harker's deputy and the Project's resident computer guru. One of the old Nike magazines contained a bank of Crays with enough computing power to rival Langley.

Harker set her pen down and looked at Selena. "You handled that attack in Paris. Are you fit to go back in the field?"

Selena had been badly wounded the year before. A bullet had clipped her spine and almost killed her. For a while, it looked like she'd be in a wheelchair for life. She hadn't been in the field since then.

Selena took a breath. She'd known this day would come.

"I still have to be careful, but yes, I can go back."

"You're sure?"

"Yes."

Harker nodded. "Good. For now, just work on the translation."

"I'd like to take the file home with me. I can get most of it figured out before I need to work with Stephanie."

"All right. Nick, you stick close to Selena, in case someone decides to make another try at the manuscript. Consider yourself a high priced bodyguard."

He smirked at Selena and stroked an imaginary moustache. "I will guard your body," he said in a deep voice.

"Jerk," she said.

CHAPTER THREE

Marcel Sarti sat on the terrace of his hillside villa on the outskirts of Marseille, savoring a pastis and watching a yacht under full sail glide across the sparkling blue waters of the Gulf of Lion. The boss of L' *Union Corse* was in a good mood. It was a beautiful day, one of those days in the south of France when everything seems possible and new. The licorice taste of the drink formed pleasant heat on his tongue.

He watched preparations for his daughter's sixteenth birthday taking place on the green lawn below. A large tent was up, the tables set, the caterers on the scene. The bar was ready. Marcel expected 200 guests. An invitation was more than an honor, it was an unspoken command. It was not wise to offend Marcel Sarti by refusing. Six of the mayors of the city's arondissments and several council members would be in attendance. The Chief of Police was expected. And of course the CEO of the Grand Port of Marseille would be there. Smooth operations at France's busiest port were essential to the flow of drugs that formed a cornerstone of Marcel Sarti's empire.

If there was one bothersome thought to spoil Sarti's day, it was his failure to secure the manuscript in Paris. Marcel didn't know who had hired him to get the book. The contract had come through an intermediary, an American he'd dealt with in the past.

The targets had turned out to be more than tourists, which complicated things. One of his contacts in the police had learned the woman was a former consultant with the American NSA and worked for one of the American intelligence services. So did the man she'd been with.

The last thing Sarti needed was to piss off NSA or the CIA. Retrieving the book was more trouble than it was worth.

He'd cancelled the contract and wired the money back to the Swiss account, less a reasonable compensation for the loss of his men. He wanted nothing more to do with it. The American had been insulting when Sarti informed him of his decision, something only a fool would do with Marcel.

He finished his pastis and stood. After the party he would decide what needed to be done about the American.

CHAPTER FOUR

Indian Island was a little over five hundred rugged acres of rock and trees, fifteen minutes by motor launch from the Maine coast. A deep cove on the leeward side formed a small, natural harbor. A long, wooden pier stretched out from the rocky shore into the water. Anchored in the cove was a white motor yacht shaped like a hunter's arrow.

The main house was a three story structure of Maine timber, built in 1851 with profits from the slave trade. A wide gallery ran around the second story. The roof was capped by a widow's walk. A manicured lawn sloped from the house to the dock, green and perfect. The lawn was bordered by beds of brilliant flowers and half a dozen trees that had been saplings when the Pilgrims landed at Plymouth Rock.

The island provided a secure setting for special events of America's ruling class. One was about to begin, the annual meeting of the Cask and Swords Society. The majority of the members would be present. They would bring their wives, their fiancées and their mistresses. There would be good food, conversations, good liquor. Important decisions would be made.

It was a perfect June morning. The caterers had almost finished setting up on the lawn. A large tent sparkled white in the morning sun. Barbecues were already smoking. Inside the house, three men sat at a table in the library. Through the library windows they could see the yacht riding at ease in the cove.

The three men were meeting to discuss progress in their plan to trigger war in the Middle East.

Phillip Harrison III owned the island. He was a wiry man in his mid-sixties. He wore a soft, casual shirt open at the collar, pressed tan slacks and comfortable Clark loafers. His face was an old New England face, a face that lacked humor, the kind of face seen in 18th Century portraits of colonial clergymen and wealthy merchants, narrow and unsmiling. Harrison had gray hair and hazel eyes and hands with long, narrow fingers. His family had controlled a large portion of America's wealth since the early days of the Republic. He owned and managed the largest private investment bank in the country. No one opened an account with his bank for less than five million dollars. Harrison considered that a small account.

Harrison often thought he would have been more at home in the 18th or 19th Century, when leaders of men were expected to apologize to no one except God for their actions. Harrison believed in God. He believed God had set him on earth to become rich and use his wealth to spread the true faith of an austere and judgmental Christianity. He believed God had given him a mission to wrest control of the Holy Land and the Middle East from Islam. It was the overriding motive in his life. It was why the three men were meeting, although they all had different reasons for wanting the same result.

The second man was Stephen Boyd. Boyd was a round-faced, round-bellied man. His features showed a hint of dissolution. His lips were distended, almost purple in color, a sign of digestive problems that sometimes embarrassed him in company. Boyd's family had been a dominant force in oil since the start of the industry in Pennsylvania. He'd been recruited into CIA right out of the University. He was currently inactive except as a deep source of information. There was no public record that his relationship with Langley had ever existed. It was better that way.

Allen Croft, the third man, owned the yacht at the end of the pier. Croft ran an international consortium of arms manufacturers. If there was a weapon in the world, one of the companies in his consortium had probably made it. He had the look of a predator, with black eyes that glittered under thick eyebrows. Women of a certain type found him attractive. For Croft, war in any part of the world was good for business. He was always looking to create new opportunities and a big, regional war was the best business opportunity of all. The one they were planning would provide handsome profits.

All three were members of Cask and Swords, a secret society that had formed in the early days of the University. Every nation in history had a ruling class based on wealth, connections and power. In America, many of that class belonged to Cask and Swords. Past and present swordsmen included presidents, cabinet officials, governors, military leaders, senators and congressmen. The financial direction of the country was currently in the hands of Cask and Swords members.

The exercise of power and the accumulation of wealth required sacrifices by the masses. The common people had never understood that, but Harrison and the others did. All three men considered it their birth right to shape the destiny of nations and wield power.

They had been making small talk while a servant laid out a light lunch and drinks. Harrison waited until the man left the room.

"The attempt to secure the Nostradamus manuscript failed," he said.

"Who did you use for the acquisition?" Croft asked.

"Marcel Sarti. The boss of *L'Union Corse*."

"I could have recommended someone better. The French mob is unreliable. They are much too crude."

"It makes no difference now. Needless to say, I am disappointed in Sarti. He had the arrogance to keep part of the fee, even though he failed. He thinks he's in control."

"What do you intend to do?" Boyd asked.

"About Sarti?" Harrison glanced at his watch, a gold Patek-Phillipe. "He won't be an annoyance much longer. I am more concerned about the manuscript. Bertrand sent it to a woman who works for the Project."

"Ah. The President's pet intelligence unit."

"Yes. She was a friend of Bertrand and happened to be visiting Paris. Bertrand sent it to her before he died. She is an accomplished martial artist. When Sarti's thugs tried to take it from her they ended up in a French hospital."

"Do you think she knows what's in the file?"

"Not yet." Harrison sipped white wine from one of his Italian vineyards. "She's an expert linguist. She'll be able to translate it. Once she does, she'll take it to her Director. It complicates things."

"What do you think they'll do?"

"I expect they'll follow up on the quatrains. It's what we'd do."

"What if they discover what we're looking for?"

"What if they do? It may work to our advantage."

Croft said, "This could all be a waste of time. I think we should go ahead with the alternative plan."

"We have to be patient," Harrison said. "It's been over 3000 years. We can wait a little longer."

"The election in Israel is getting closer and Weisner is still behind in the polls."

"As I said, Arthur, be patient. An opportunity will present itself, one way or another. If we need to take a different approach, we will. Everything is in place. It's much better if it works out the way we hope. The discovery will make Weisner a popular hero in Israel. His election will be assured. The rest will follow."

Boyd took a sip of water. "The EPA is causing trouble for me again. President Rice takes the law seriously."

"When the war starts there won't be any more problems with the EPA. Rice will need the oil." Harrison said.

The men began eating.

CHAPTER FIVE

Marcel Sarti stepped out of his favorite restaurant into the Marseilles evening, lit a Gitane and gave a deep sigh of satisfaction. Blue smoke from the cigarette curled upward in lazy spirals in the still air. From here Marcel was heading to one of his clubs, where there were discrepancies in the finances. Sarti didn't like discrepancies. He'd found out who was responsible and now intended to send a graphic message to anyone else who might have creative accounting ideas. For the moment, he was enjoying the night air and the afterglow of an excellent meal. The unpleasantness to come would keep a little longer. A bodyguard stood by the open door of Sarti's black Mercedes.

Down the street, two men sat on a dark blue BMW motorcycle. The bike idled with a soft rumble. The passenger held a MAC-10 machine pistol concealed under his jacket. Both men wore full face black helmets with smoked visors. The man at the controls was named Eric. The man with the gun was called Peter.

They watched Sarti emerge from the restaurant and light his cigarette.

"There he is."

Peter slipped the gun from under the jacket. Eric put the BMW in gear and pulled away from the curb.

Sarti glanced over at the motorcycle as it came alongside the Mercedes. Peter raised the gun and fired a long burst. The sound ripped a hole through the night. A bright red pattern appeared on Sarti's elegant yellow silk shirt. The cigarette fell from his fingers. He pitched forward onto the sidewalk.

The bodyguard fired as the bike went past, the shots echoing off the apartment buildings lining the street. The bike swerved. Peter grunted and let off another burst. The guard stumbled and fell. Eric twisted the throttle and the bike roared away.

Half an hour later, the BMW was parked in a rented garage on the outskirts of the city. The space was lit by a single, fly-specked bulb hanging from the ceiling. Peter lay on the oil-stained cement floor, his jacket slick with blood. The round had gone in low on the side. He'd managed to stay on the bike until they'd reached the garage. Now he was in shock, half conscious. His face looked white and pinched in the weak light. Blood leaked out from under him. Eric took out a cell phone and called.

"It's done," he said. "There was trouble."

"What trouble?"

"Peter is badly wounded. He needs a hospital."

"That's not possible."

"I know."

"You know what to do. Get back to the Embassy." The call ended.

Eric turned off his phone and knelt down next to the man on the floor. It was too bad, he'd started to like him.

"I'm sorry," he said. His voice was soft.

The knife was a silver flash in his hand. He drove it up under the sternum and twisted. Blood gushed from Peter's mouth. His eyes went wide, shocked. The body went rigid, then settled into stillness. A sewer stench filled the room.

Eric stood. He wiped off the knife on Peter's shirt and put it back in his pocket. He left the garage by a side door and walked to a car parked nearby. In six or seven hours he would be in Paris. By the time the police found the bike and the body he would be out of the country. The authorities would assume Sarti's death was part of a struggle for control of L'Union Corse. They would assume the dead man had been killed to keep him silent.

They would be right about that part, but they would never know the real reason behind the night's work.

CHAPTER SIX

The pages of the Nostradamus file were spread out on a work table in Selena's luxurious Washington condo. Nick spent a lot of time here, but he'd kept his apartment. Every time he thought about moving in with her, something held him back. Selena hadn't pushed for something more permanent. Whether that was because she was afraid of what would happen if she did or if she was as wary as he was, he didn't know. They didn't talk about it.

Lately, it felt as if something was changing between them. A sense of distance. He couldn't put his finger on what it was, exactly. Just a feeling. Sometimes he thought being with her was like being one of those rubber balls on a paddle that kept bouncing away and coming back again.

He looked at the manuscript pages on the table. Someone had tried to stick a knife in him on a Paris street because of them. Selena's friend was dead, because of them. What made them worth killing for?

"Do you think Nostradamus could really see the future?"

She brushed her hand across her forehead. "People have argued about that since the prophecies were published in 1555. A few seem to predict real events. Listen to these two."

She read from her notes.

An island in the New World: Danger
The young Eagle stands before the Bear
Thunder over the waters
Shadows beneath the sea, more fierce than dragons

"So?" Nick said.

"The bear is a symbol of Russia. It was like that even back then. I think this is about the Cuban Missile crisis in 1962. The eagle and the bear could be America and Russia. Thunder over the waters could be jets. And shadows beneath the sea could refer to submarines."

"You think he predicted an event 400 years in the future?"

"It's possible. He predicted the rise and fall of Hitler and the Nazis. If he got Hitler right, why not Cuba and the Russians?"

"Maybe. You said two. What's the other one?"

The Sun touches the Earth
In an instant, all is gone
The people of the land
Cry unheeded to the flower throne

"There's only one flower throne," she said, "the Chrysanthemum throne in Japan. That would make this about Hiroshima. You could make a case that the Japanese people were unheeded by the Emperor after the bomb was dropped. It took the second one before Hirohito gave up."

She looked at the pages. "I've translated two more but they don't make much sense." She picked up a piece of paper covered with notes and handed it to him.

A dark prince seeks this which is stolen
With the sound of trumpets
The golden cherubim shake the heavens
They will stand or fall, the outcome in doubt

Where water is bartered as gold
A small castle guards treasure beyond price
A cross and dome point the way
Beware the Red Horseman

"None of these make any sense," Nick said. "A dark prince. He could be talking about Darth Vader, for all we know. You can interpret these any way you like."

Selena smiled. "That's always been a problem with the good doctor."

"Nostradamus was a doctor?"

"Sort of. He never graduated from medical school. He was famous for treating the plague, but his cures didn't work very well."

"You look like you're enjoying this," he said.

She nodded. "It's exciting. Do you realize what it's like for me, having this to work with?"

"Do you realize what it's like for me, to have you wrapped up in a 16th Century manuscript?"

She laughed. "Maybe I should take a break."

"How about dinner at that new Indian restaurant?"

"I'm not very hungry."

"We could do something to work up an appetite before we go out."

"What did you have in mind?"

"I have to show you."

He led her into the bedroom. They kissed. Selena started to unbutton her blouse. She stopped.

"Oh," she said.

Nick was about to take off his shirt. He stopped, his hand on his belt. "What?"

"I just thought of something."

She left the bedroom, doing up buttons.

Nick stood by the empty bed for a moment. There was a downside to living with Selena's mind. He sighed and followed her into the other room. She went to a bookcase and pulled out a Bible and walked over to the table with the manuscript. She sat down and began turning pages in the Bible.

"What are you doing?"

"I had an idea about what Jean-Paul meant when he wrote EX 25. It could be a biblical reference."

She found Exodus and turned pages to Chapter 25. "Oh, my," she said.

CHAPTER SEVEN

Former gunnery sergeant Ronnie Peete, USMC, sat on the couch in Harker's office with Lamont and Stephanie. He had on one of his quieter Hawaiian shirts, a scene of white and red flowers on a light brown background. The shirt almost picked up the tint of his skin. Ronnie was Navajo, raised on the reservation in Arizona. He had a large nose and dark brown eyes. People thought of paintings and photographs of the Old West when they saw Ronnie, unless he was holding a weapon pointed at them.

Ronnie looked relaxed. Lamont looked like a piece of spring steel. His eyes were icy blue, a mark of his Ethiopian ancestry. There was a thin scar of pink tissue across his face from a shrapnel wound he'd gotten in Iraq. Sometimes young children stared wide-eyed and clung to their mothers when he walked by. It hurt his feelings, but there wasn't much he could do about it.

Harker cleared her throat. "Interpol confirmed that Bertrand was offering the Nostradamus manuscript on the black market. He put it up on a hidden website that can only be accessed by people with the right code."

She brought the page up on the big wall monitor.

"This is the announcement. It's still up. Interpol is using it as bait."

It was written in English, French, German, Russian and Chinese. They read it in silence.

For the discriminating collector: a unique opportunity to acquire the legendary lost quatrains of the Seventh Century of Les Propheties by Michele de Nostradamus. An original manuscript in the Seer's own hand.

Guaranteed authentic.

A photograph of the quatrain about the cherubim was prominently featured. Selena sighed, a sound of disappointment.

Jean-Paul, she thought. *What happened, to make you do this?*

"So now we know how the bad guys knew about it," Nick said.

Harker continued. "Someone killed the boss of the French Mafia yesterday. His name was Sarti. He was a major player in stolen antiquities. My intuition says it's related to Bertrand's death."

Nick scratched his ear. Harker's intuition was usually dead on. "What do the French think?"

"That Bertrand's death happened during a robbery and Sarti was killed because of a power struggle within the mob. They found the body of Sarti's killer. He was wounded by Sarti's bodyguard but someone else killed him, probably to keep him quiet. Interpol doesn't much care if the bad guys kill each other and they're not pursuing it. The French are watching to see who takes Sarti's place, but that's all."

"Any ID on the shooter?"

"That's interesting. He was American, former Special Forces."

"A mercenary? What would an American be doing working for the French Mafia? They have their own shooters. That doesn't make sense." Nick paused. "Maybe someone hired Sarti to get the manuscript and it pissed them off when he didn't come through, so they got even."

"Kind of extreme," Ronnie said.

"So was killing Bertrand."

"Selena, what have you found out?" Harker asked.

"The manuscript is definitely by Nostradamus. It's not complete, but it's part of the quatrains no one has seen before. Jean-Paul would have been able to read them." She paused. "I think I know why he was killed. It ties into the letters and number he scrawled on the floor."

"E X 25."

"EX 25 is a biblical reference. Exodus, Chapter 25."

Harker was getting impatient. Her pen began its drumbeat on her desk. Nick waited. He knew what was coming.

"What does that have to do with the manuscript?"

"Chapter 25 describes God's instructions to Moses for building the Ark of the Covenant. Nostradamus knew where it was hidden."

Harker's pen stopped moving. *That got her attention*, Nick thought.

"Are you telling me those pages hold the key to the location of the Ark of the Covenant?"

"Nostradamus thought so. So did Jean-Paul. So far I've found one quatrain that could be about the Ark. There are three more grouped with it, but I'm not sure what they mean."

She read them out loud.

A dark prince seeks this which is stolen
With the sound of trumpets
The golden cherubim shake the heavens
They will stand or fall, the outcome in doubt

In the land of Moab where Moses stood
Two kneel at the feet of the shepherd
Five signs mark the path
If no one follows, a terrible fate

That which was sought was not found
Fire and death no tongue would loosen
In the land of the fair king
The Pale Rider reigns supreme

Where water is bartered as gold
A small castle guards treasure beyond price

A cross and dome point the way
Beware the Red Horseman

"That's it?" Harker said.

Selena nodded. "Some of it is clear. The golden cherubim fits the biblical description of the Ark. I don't know what he means by 'shake the heavens'. The Pale Rider is the first of the Four Horsemen of the Apocalypse."

"Pale Rider. Clint Eastwood," Lamont said. "I saw that. Good movie."

Everyone looked at him.

"What?"

Harker sighed. "Go on, Selena."

"The Red Horseman is War. He's the second of the Four Horsemen in Revelations."

"Nostradamus was a cheerful kind of guy, wasn't he?" Lamont said.

Selena ignored him. "The land of Moab is modern day Jordan. Mount Nebo is where Moses stood when God showed him the Promised land. I don't know what the five signs are, or the shepherd. Nostradamus is saying bad things will happen if someone doesn't figure it out. Maybe that's us."

Stephanie said, "Then the Ark is on Mt. Nebo?"

Stephanie's voice was soft. She wore a dark blue skirt and blouse. Large gold hoops dangled from her ears. Her brown eyes reminded Nick of a doe. Unlike a doe, Steph had a pistol in a quick draw holster at her waist and knew how to use it. She had a quick intelligence and a genius ability with computers.

"I don't think it's still on Mount Nebo, if it ever was," Selena said.

"The Ark of the Covenant could cause serious problems in the wrong hands," Harker said. "The real article could light a fire in the Middle East. If it exists, we have to find it."

"You really think it's that important?" Lamont said.

"The Ark is sacred to the three major Western religions. Of course it's important, it could start a war. The whole Middle East is ready to explode, right now. There's the Israeli election, the problems with Syria, the rhetoric out of Iran. The discovery of the Ark could be the last straw. This has to be why people are getting murdered over that manuscript."

She tapped her pen, thinking. "If we can get an idea of where it is, I'm going to send the team after it."

"You're going to send us after the Ark of the Covenant?" Nick said. "Do I look like Harrison Ford?"

"Maybe with the right hat."

Everyone laughed.

"Do I get a bullwhip?"

"No. You get a SIG .40. I want everyone to switch over. The guns are already downstairs in the armory. I know you like your .45, Nick, but I want everyone carrying the same thing. We have to standardize."

"I'd rather keep my H-K."

"It's not open to discussion. You want the .45, take it as backup." She fixed him with one of her *don't mess with me* looks. He decided to let it pass for the moment.

"Where do you want us to begin looking?"

"Jordan. Go to Mount Nebo and see if you can find those five signs."

"I need to finish translating the manuscript before we go anywhere," Selena said.

"How long will it take?"

"I don't know. Steph and I are going to work on it when we're done here."

Harker looked at her. "You said some of the quatrains were missing."

"That's right."

"Could Bertrand have had them?"

"If he did, why not send them to me with the rest?" Selena brushed a hair from her forehead.

"You told me he was paranoid," Nick said. "He could have split the file up, sent one part to you, one to someone else. "

"Maybe it's still in his shop."

"The police have been all through the shop," Harker said. "There's nothing like that."

"Where else would he send it?" Ronnie asked Selena. "Family, someone like that? Maybe a lawyer?"

"He had a lawyer. No family, though."

Harker made a note. "What's the lawyer's name?"

"I met him, once." Selena frowned, trying to remember the name. "Durand, that's it. Jacques Durand. He's in Paris."

"Let's look him up." Harker said. She pulled a hidden keyboard out of her desk and tapped a key. The wall monitor lit. She entered Jacques Durand + Lawyer + Paris in a Google search.

The top hit was a headline. *French mob lawyer found murdered*.

Harker clicked on the link. It was a newspaper article from the day before. Durand had been working late when someone had killed him. His office had been ransacked. Police were investigating. Durand had defended members of L'Union Corse in the past. The article speculated on a possible link to the death of Marcel Sarti and suggested that a gang war had started.

"Someone else thinks like we do," Nick said. "This can't be a coincidence. They were looking for the manuscript."

Elizabeth said, "I wonder if the lawyer had the other part? If there is one."

Nick tugged on his left ear, where a Chinese bullet had taken off most of the earlobe. His ear was a built-in genetic warning system. It itched and burned when things were about to get dicey. They all knew it. He saw the look the others gave him.

"Just an itch," he said.

"I wish you wouldn't do that when it doesn't count," Lamont said.

"You want me to just let it itch?"

"Better than getting everybody upset."

"That's enough, Lamont." Harker picked up her pen. "Selena, where else could it be if the lawyer didn't have it?"

"Jean-Paul had a country house in Provence, in the south of France. I think there was a housekeeper who took care of it when he wasn't there."

"He could have mailed it to himself at the house," Ronnie said. "The cops wouldn't turn that up when they checked the messenger services."

Harker's intuition was setting off alarms. It rarely failed her. No one outside of the Project knew she sometimes used intuition to make major decisions. Intuition wasn't high on the list of acknowledged intelligence analysis skills. She made a decision now.

She turned to Nick and Selena. "Go to France and check out that house. See if something's there. You can go on to Jordan after that."

"The French cops are pissed at us," Nick said. "We'll never get out of the airport."

"Don't worry about that. Take your weapons. I'll clear it with the French."

Nick scratched his ear.

CHAPTER EIGHT

They flew into Paris and on to Avignon. Harker had called in a favor so they could carry their pistols. They rented a white Renault and headed for the vacation retreat of Jean-Paul Bertrand.

The first part of the drive passed in silence.

The melody of a folk song was stuck in Nick's head.

Joshua fit the battle of Jericho, Jericho, Jericho
Joshua fit the battle of Jericho
And the walls come a-tumblin' down.

"Damn song is driving me crazy," he said.

"What song?"

"The one about Joshua and the battle of Jericho."

She hummed a few bars. "All I can remember is the chorus."

"Yeah. It wouldn't be so bad if I could think of the rest of the words."

"Something about Joshua and the trumpets blowing, I think."

"The Ark was at the battle of Jericho," Nick said. "That's what made me think of the song. I wonder how Joshua knocked down those walls? Jericho was impregnable, the ultimate fortress of its time."

"All that history is lost, except for Bible stories."

Nick scratched his ear. "You think God knocked the walls down to help Joshua out?"

"I believe in God. I don't believe God intervenes like that. I think it's a teaching story based on the actual battle. But those walls were real. I don't think Joshua's army could have

smashed through them without something we don't
understand."

"Like a secret weapon."

"Yes. The Bible says the priests carried the Ark around the
walls blowing horns for six days and on the seventh day the
wall came down. Maybe they had something that amplified
those horns."

"In the Ark?"

"Sound at the right frequency will shatter stone. In terms
of modern technology, that would make sense."

"3000 years ago isn't modern."

"No one will ever know how they did it." Selena had her
GPS out. "Take the next right, up ahead."

The road became a narrow lane between low stone walls
covered with vines.

"Slow down," she said. "The entrance is coming up on the
left."

They turned onto a long, straight drive of crushed rock
lined with trees. Stunted oaks and juniper and grass fanned out
on both sides. The grass was green and tall, dotted with yellow
and blue flowers.

The house was a single story made of stone, washed white
in the afternoon sunlight, with a tiled roof and covered porch. It
seemed like part of the natural landscape, a house out of
another time. Nick could imagine Cezanne or Van Gogh
painting in the back yard.

"Nice," he said.

"It was a farmer's cottage in the old days. Jean-Paul
renovated it. I've never been here, but he talked about it a lot.
He loved it."

"I can see why."

Nick parked. They got out and walked to the porch.

"The door's open," he said.

Both reached for their pistols at the same time. Nick
nudged the door with his foot. It swung inward. He couldn't see
anyone inside, but he could see the mess.

It only took a minute to clear the house. There was a bathroom, a bedroom and a combined kitchen and living area. A back porch looked out over a garden and a small, natural pool shaded by oaks. No one was there.

Books and papers were scattered about the living area. Drawers had been pulled out and dumped on the floor. There was a broken vase by the door, knocked off a side table.

"Seems like someone is always one step ahead of us," Nick said.

Selena looked out the window. "There's a car coming."

An old Citroen 2CV came up the drive, trailing blue smoke. The wheels crunched on the rock. They watched it from the living room.

"Maybe the bad guys missed something," Nick said.

"I don't think the Mafia would drive around in something like that," she said.

"You're a car snob. Maybe it's all they could find."

The Citroen parked next to their rented Renault. A woman got out of the car. She was dressed in a purple, flowery print dress that bagged loosely around her body. A bandana was wrapped around hennaed hair damaged by too many trips to the beauty parlor. She was around fifty, plump, with swarthy skin. She wore white plastic sandals. She reached inside the car and brought out a basket. Nick could see spray bottles sticking out and a roll of paper towels. He put his pistol away.

"Cleaning lady, looks like." He stepped out on the porch with Selena.

"*Bonjour, Madame,*" Selena said.

"*Bonjour.*" The woman reached inside the basket and took out a Swedish machine pistol and pointed it at them. "Get on your knees," she said in English. "Now."

Selena looked at Nick. "I don't think she's here to clean."

Another car pulled into the drive, this one a black Mercedes. "That the right kind of car?" Nick said to Selena.

"Shut up," the cleaning lady said. "Put your hands up. Get on your knees or I shoot."

They got on their knees, hands in the air. The Mercedes stopped. Two men got out of the car. One was tall and thin, one short and squat. They wore casual clothes that looked expensive. Guns came out, pointed at Nick and Selena.

"They're armed," the woman said. "The man has a shoulder holster."

The tall one spoke. "Take out your weapons and put them on the ground. Be very careful. Do it slowly."

He's American, Nick thought. *From somewhere on the East Coast.*

"Selena, do as he says. Remember how we did it in Mali."

"Shut up. Take out the guns. Two fingers."

Nick took out his new SIG-Sauer, holding it by the butt between his thumb and finger. He laid it on the porch. Selena did the same.

"Very good. Get up. Keep your hands in the air."

They stood, slowly.

"Kick the guns away."

They kicked them off the porch. The cleaning lady lowered the barrel of her gun and moved behind the others. The two men stepped onto the porch. Short Man had plastic ties in one hand, his pistol in the other.

"Turn around," the tall one said. "Put your hands behind you."

They turned. Short Man stepped close.

Selena moved first. She whirled and knocked the gun from his hand. It went off, sending a flock of birds shrieking into the sky. She slammed the edge of her rigid palm against his neck, harder than she'd meant. Something broke.

Tall Man hadn't expected trouble. He froze for an instant. It was enough.

Nick swept the gun away with a quick crossing motion of his hands and moved in. The pistol fired into the ground. He drove his knuckled fist into Tall Man's throat, a killing blow to the larynx. The cleaning lady brought up her gun. The man clutched at his throat, trying to breathe. His face went purple.

Nick pushed him off the porch into the cleaning lady as she fired, using him for a shield. The bullets hit him in the back. The woman fell backward with both men on top of her. Nick reached past the dead man and slammed his fist into her face, brought his hand up and struck down across the bridge of her nose. It shattered. She screamed curses at him, trying to bring her gun to bear, firing into the air. He hit her again, a hammer blow. She fell silent.

On the porch, the second man lay dead. Nick got to his feet.

"Mali?" Selena said.

"Maybe not exactly the same. But you knew what I meant."

In Mali, they'd been attacked on the street. Selena's martial arts had kept them alive.

"Yes. I did."

"Did you mean to kill him?" he asked.

"No. But he asked for it."

She'd changed a lot since Nick had met her. Two years with the Project had stripped away most of her hesitation about hurting people who tried to hurt her. It was a question of survival. You couldn't hesitate. The second man had hesitated, which was why he was dead.

Nick said, "We'd better get out of here."

"Shouldn't we keep searching?"

"If anything was here, they've already got it."

"What about her?"

The cleaning lady was unconscious. Her face was covered in blood.

"She can clean up after herself."

They got in the car and drove away.

CHAPTER NINE

Nick dreamed.

He's in the village again, where a child will die. On the right are the flat roofed houses that will turn into platforms of death for his Marines. On the left, more houses and a patchwork of ramshackle bins and hanging cloth walls that make up the market. Flies buzz in clouds around meat hanging in the butcher's stall.

He hears a baby cry. He always hears the baby cry, somewhere in one of the houses, a thin, frightened wail. The street is deserted.

The enemy rises up on the rooftops and begins firing, like always. The market stalls turn into a firestorm of splinters and plaster and rock exploding from the sides of the buildings, like always.

A child runs at him from one of the houses, yelling that God is Great. He can't be more than ten or eleven years old. The boy cocks his arm back and throws the grenade. Nick's rifle kicks back in a quick 3 round burst and the child's face disappears in a plume of blood. The grenade drifts through the air in slow motion...everything goes white...

"Nick!"

Selena's voice woke him. They were in a hotel in Paris. He sat upright, heart pounding as if it would smash through his ribs. He wiped his hand across his face, rubbed his eyes. The dreams had come back, more frequent since the attack on the old Project building. Always some variation of the same dream, reliving the day he'd almost died. The day he'd shot a child.

Selena stood naked by the side of the bed. She didn't look happy.

"Why are you out of bed?"

"You hit me in your sleep, thrashing around. I got out of the way."

"Oh, hell. I'm sorry."

"You have to do something about this. It's getting worse. We've talked about it before. You have to see someone."

Nick was silent.

"I know you don't want to talk with a therapist. But you have to do it. For both of us. You have to see someone."

"All right. I'll think about it."

She sat down on the bed. "Promise me, Nick. Promise you'll do it."

"I said I'd think about it."

"Promise you'll do it."

There was something unspoken in her voice, a warning.

"Okay," he said. "I'll do it. After we get back." He looked at the clock. "It's too early to get up," he said.

She moved next to him. "We don't need to get up."

She touched his face, ran her fingers over the stubble.

"I don't think I can go back to sleep," he said.

"We don't have to sleep."

Selena moved her hand down his side, feeling the old scars, the legacy of war written on his body.

"Besides," she said, "if you're not asleep, I don't have to duck."

He looked into her eyes, felt the smooth curve of her hip.

Later, they slept.

CHAPTER TEN

Nick and Selena took an Air France flight from Paris to Amman in Jordan, rented a Land Rover at the airport and drove to the American embassy. Harker had arranged for their guns to be forwarded from the embassy in Paris. It was a handy use for the diplomatic pouch.

They picked up the guns and went to their hotel. It was situated on the highest hill in Amman, looking out over the city in a spectacular view. Tall, Romanesque columns scaled the facade. A row of palms marched along the street in front of the building. The lobby featured a huge central display of purple and white flowers. It was the kind of hotel where everything was marble and polished wood, where you felt like you were worth a million. In Selena's case, she was. Her uncle's death two years before had left her a rich woman.

The next day they set off for Mount Nebo, 40 kilometers south of Amman. The road south was modern blacktop, busy with heavy truck traffic. The Land Rover ran smoothly over the pavement.

The day was hot and clear. Once out of the city, the desert stretched in all directions, a harsh landscape of sand and rock that sent shimmering heat ripples into the air under the brilliant sun. Selena wore a loose blue scarf around her neck and a white cotton blouse that set off her tan. There was a brown leather pouch on her belt. A calf-length cotton skirt and hiking boots completed the outfit. The gun was tucked away in the pouch. Her violet eyes were hidden behind dark brown sunglasses. Wind from the open window ruffled her hair.

Nick had opted for jeans, a short-sleeved shirt and a light jacket to conceal his holster. He wore Ray-Bans against the relentless light. The air smelled of the desert, dry and clean. *It probably smelled like this when Moses was here*, he thought.

"We're right in the heart of the Old Testament," Selena said. "Moses is supposed to be buried where we're going, on Mount Nebo. This whole area was fought over for centuries. The Israelites, the Moabites, the Ammonites, the Byzantines, the Nabateans."

"You wonder why," Nick said. "Who would want it? This is a desolate place. Look at it. Sand, rock, sun. Hell, the nearest water is the Dead Sea. Reminds me of parts of Utah or Nevada."

"You won't find anything like Las Vegas here," she said.

They turned west at Madaba, a town famous for elaborate Byzantine mosaics. From there it was another ten kilometers to Mount Nebo. The road leading up the mountain was paved in a herring bone pattern of gray-blue and light stone, bordered by stone curbing and tall Eucalyptus trees on both sides.

They had come to one of the most famous places in the Bible.

They parked and walked the rest of the way to the top, where a chapel had been built in the 4th Century CE to commemorate the death of Moses. A Byzantine church had followed two hundred years later. Now it was a Franciscan monastery, a focal point of anger for the Muslim extremists. A shelter had been erected over the ruins of the old church to form the new Memorial Chapel.

A low wall of limestone blocks marked the edge of the summit. A tall, modern sculpture of Moses' staff rose like a silent sentinel into the sky. Before them stretched the desert battleground of the three great Western religions.

The Holy Land.

"Hell of a view," Nick said. "You can see all the way to Jerusalem from here."

"Is that all you can say?" she said. "A hell of a view?" She shook her head.

"What do you expect me to say? All I know is that a lot of people died here for thousands of years because they had different names for God. They're still dying. It's as senseless now as it was back then."

Selena changed the subject. She pointed to the left at a large body of water. "That's the Dead Sea. And over there you can just make out the West Bank of the Jordan."

The sun beat down on them, hot and searing. "It does give you a sense of history," Nick said. "Imagine walking through that wasteland thousands of years ago. It must have been tough."

"Let's look inside the church."

They walked to the building. Nick stopped and bent down to tie his boot. "Don't look around. We're being followed. There's a man wearing a yellow shirt and a ball cap behind us. He was at the airport and I saw him again at the hotel."

"He could be a tourist," she said. "We're not the only ones that want to come here."

"Maybe."

They stepped out of the bright sun into the cool shade of the chapel. It was open on the sides. The limestone ruins and broken columns of the original building were covered by a wide, modern roof. A dozen flat wooden benches were placed on each side of a mosaic tile walkway decorated with repeating rows of peacocks. Sunlight streamed through windows in the roof, making the stones glow with soft color. Broken columns lined the side of the aisle.

"This is beautiful," Nick said.

Selena was surprised. She hadn't expected him to say that. "Yes, it is."

"There's something about the light on the stone that makes this place feel peaceful."

She touched his arm. It was a good feeling, something they felt together. Nick smiled.

At the far end was a simple altar made of stone. An ancient mosaic cross was set into the wall above it, a symmetrical design of interweaving loops. To the right of the altar was another area with a mosaic floor. A sign said it had been laid down in the 6th Century.

The tile floor showed two men with animals on ropes. One man led an ostrich, the other a zebra and a spotted camel. Above the men was a shepherd under some trees, with a goat and sheep. At the top of the mosaic, another shepherd fought a lioness and a soldier hunted a lion.

"That's some floor," Nick said.

"Kneel at the feet of the shepherd," she said. She got down on her knees. Nick watched her. He looked at the floor.

"There are five trees where you're kneeling."

"You're right."

"That could be the five signs Nostradamus meant."

"Five trees? That doesn't tell us much."

"Why would he make it easy? Maybe it's about something besides trees."

She climbed to her feet. "We'd better see if anything else fits."

They spent the next two hours exploring and found nothing that hinted at the Ark or five signs. Aside from the view, the chapel and the mosaics, there wasn't a lot to see. The man with the ball cap was nowhere in sight. Nick decided he was just being paranoid. It was an old habit.

"Let's go back to the hotel," Selena said. "I need my laptop and an internet connection to research those trees. They must mean something."

They got in their car and drove back down the mountain. The man in the yellow shirt and ball cap watched them go. Then he took out his phone and made a call.

CHAPTER ELEVEN

Selena had been on her computer for almost an hour.

"I know what the five trees stand for but I'm not sure it helps much."

Nick waited for her to explain.

"It's a Gnostic symbol. There are several possible meanings. One is that they symbolize purification of the five senses, a metaphor for gaining union with God. Jesus is supposed to have said there are five trees in paradise and that whoever knows them will find eternal life. You come across it in the Gospel of Thomas and other Gnostic texts."

"I don't remember a Gospel of Thomas."

"It's one of several books that were kept out of the Bible."

"Why didn't they keep it?"

"It doesn't tell the same story as the others. The Gnostic texts were all considered heretical. They tell a different story. Gnostics believed in a direct knowledge of God. No intermediaries."

"No priests?"

"Right. If you're building a church where you want to be in charge, you can't have people deciding on their own what God wants. You need to make sure someone acts as the middle man."

"So young and yet so cynical," Nick said.

She shrugged. "I didn't come up with that idea. Anyway, that's what the trees symbolize."

"That still doesn't tell us where to look."

"What if we're on the wrong track about the trees?"

"What do you mean?"

"I've been thinking the clue was what the trees symbolized. That doesn't lead anywhere useful. Now I think Nostradamus meant something else. I still think the trees are the five signs in the quatrain."

Nick got up and looked out the hotel window at Amman. "Okay." he said over his shoulder. "If it's not what the trees mean as a symbol, why write a quatrain about them?"

"To draw attention to the shepherd?"

"The shepherd is just a shepherd. You kneel there and see the trees. The trees are part of the mosaic. What else is there, if it's not the trees?"

"The animals," she said. "The zebra and lion and the others."

He turned back to face her. "African animals. Maybe Nostradamus means that the Ark is in Africa."

"Ethiopia," she said. "The city of Axum. There's a chapel that's supposed to hold the Ark."

"I've heard of that," Nick said. "If it's there, it isn't lost, is it?" Nick pulled up a chair next to her and sat down. "We don't know anything. We can't run around Africa looking for this. Let's make some assumptions."

"Feel free."

"The first assumption is that the quatrain is a genuine clue to the location of the Ark, right?"

"If it isn't, we've wasted a lot of time."

"Tell me a little more about Nostradamus."

"Like what?"

"You said he always hid the real meaning of his quatrains because he was afraid of persecution."

"Yes. That's why it's so hard to interpret them."

"Did he mention specific places like Mount Nebo in the prophecies?"

"Often."

"Were those places symbolic?"

"Sometimes. What are you getting at?"

"What is it that's important about Mount Nebo?" Nick said.

"It's where Moses was shown the Promised Land by God, and where he's buried. I don't see where you're going with this."

"What if the clue isn't about the trees, but about Moses as the shepherd of his people?"

"You think the shepherd in the mosaic is Moses?"

"No. I think Nostradamus wanted to make the association with Moses."

"How does that help?"

"What's the first thing you think of when you think of Moses?"

"That's easy," Selena said. "The Ten Commandments."

"Right. He gets the Commandments from God and then eventually he gets to Mount Nebo. The clue is about Moses. That's assumption number two."

Selena looked at him. "You could have been a preacher," she said. "All this biblical thinking. But I still don't get it."

"Assumption number three is that the clue is really about the Ten Commandments. Where Moses received them."

"He got them on Mount Sinai. You're saying that you think the Ark is on Mount Sinai?"

"If not the Ark, then a clue to where it is."

"Nick, that's a real stretch. Besides, even if you're right there's a complication."

"There's always a complication. What is it?"

"No one is sure exactly which mountain is the one where Moses got the Commandments. Assuming the whole story isn't just a story."

"It's not in Egypt, on the Sinai Peninsula?"

"A lot of biblical archeologists don't think so. I don't see how the Ark could be there anyway. That's one of the most picked over mountains in the world."

"Then where else would it be?" Nick said.

"When you read Exodus it says there was thunder and lightning and a cloud of smoke on the mountain."

"That sounds like someone writing in a little dramatic effect."

"But what if it wasn't for effect? What kind of mountain has smoke and thunder?"

"A volcano. Are there any volcanoes in Egypt?"
"No. But there are in Saudi Arabia," Selena said.

CHAPTER TWELVE

Nick had Harker on the satellite phone. He told her what they'd figured out.

"Come home," she said. "Something like this needs planning."

"Then you're going to send us after it?" Nick asked.

"I'll think about it. Come home." She ended the call.

"Pack your bag," Nick said to Selena.

"She wants us back in the States? What about the Ark?"

"We need a mission plan. I'll call the desk and tell them we're leaving."

Ten minutes later they walked out of the entrance to the hotel. A taxi pulled up. They got into the back seat.

"The American Embassy," Nick said, "then the airport." They needed to leave their weapons behind before they got on a plane.

The cab pulled away. Nick and Selena were quiet in the back seat. Nick watched the streets of Amman roll by. After a few minutes he said, "This isn't the way to the Embassy."

"Are you sure? We don't know the city."

"I'm sure. Driver," Nick said. "Where are you going?"

The driver was middle eastern looking, which was no surprise. He wore a skullcap. He had black hair and dark brown, liquid eyes and a beard. He looked at Nick in his mirror. "American Embassy, no worry. I take short cut, save you money."

They entered a run-down district. The streets were narrow, the houses crowded close to the road. The walls were scrawled with graffiti and crude flags. There were no westerners about. The cab slowed for people in the street. Faces turned as they passed, peering in at the foreigners. Their expressions were unfriendly. Nick's ear began itching.

He leaned over to Selena and spoke in a low voice. "It's trouble. Get ready to bail out of the car. Don't shoot unless you have to."

She nodded and slipped her pistol from her belt pack.

The street opened onto a large square surrounded by low hills. A white mosque with a tall minaret dominated one of the slopes. Shops, houses and stalls lined the sides of the square. Yellow signs and green banners with Arabic writing hung from the buildings.

They moved into the square. The driver slammed on the brakes and had his door open and was out and running before Nick could react. A white Volkswagen burst into the square from the street on Selena's side of the car. A blue Toyota pickup came at them from the street ahead. A van entered the square behind them.

People began running away.

It wasn't a good sign.

"Out!" Nick yelled.

He rolled out of the car. The Volkswagen sped toward them. Someone leaned out and opened fire with a machine pistol. Selena ducked down. The bullets shattered the windows of the taxi and sprayed fragments of glass over the pavement. She wormed her way across the back seat and dropped onto the ground next to Nick. Someone with an AK reached out of the passenger window of the Toyota coming at them. Nick fired three quick rounds. The windshield starred and the man snapped back in his seat. His gun went flying. The Toyota kept coming.

Nick entered the zone.

Everything slowed to a crawl. He could hear Selena firing at the Volkswagen, the sound rhythmic, steady, muffled as if underwater. Nick aimed at the windshield of the Toyota coming at him and began squeezing off rounds. He watched the barrel of his pistol rise with each shot, the slide come back, the

*ejected case float through the air. He heard the flat sound as
each bullet hit the windshield. The pistol locked open.*

The Toyota veered left and plowed through a fruit stall and
rammed into a house. The front end crumpled. A tongue of
flame shot out from underneath. Then the gas tank exploded in
a sudden orange cloud of flame. Bits of melon and wood and
glass and metal rained down on the square.

Time sped up again. Selena slapped in a new magazine.
Bursts of automatic fire came from the white Volkswagen,
stopped fifty feet away. The taxi rocked from the impact,
echoed with sharp, metallic sounds. Two tires blew out. The
car dropped hard to the right. The van from behind bore down
on them. Nick reached for a fresh magazine. They were out of
time, with no place to hide.

Someone leaned out of the van and sent a long burst into
the Volkswagen. The windows exploded. A red mist covered
the inside of the windshield. The van braked next to them and a
side door flew open. A man called Nick by name.

"Carter. Get in. Now." Another man inside the van fired
past him at the Volkswagen.

"What...?"

"We're friends. Get in!"

Another truck with shouting gunmen entered the square.
Nick jumped into the van, Selena right behind him. The driver
pulled into a tight U turn and headed out of the square the way
they'd come in.

The man who'd spoken said something in a foreign
language to the driver. Then he turned to Nick. "They're
coming after us. Stay down, we'll handle it."

The second man lifted an assault rifle with a grenade
launcher under the barrel. Nick pulled Selena down on the
floor. The rear doors banged open against the side of the van.
The grenade shot out the back and straight at the front of the
oncoming truck. Nick saw the driver's face go wide with fear

as he saw it come straight at him. Then it exploded and the truck was in flames. The sound echoed along the narrow street.

They drove away, a column of black smoke rising behind them. One of the men leaned out and pulled the doors shut. Nick sat up against the side of the van.

"Jesus," he said.

"Maybe not," Selena said. "They're Israeli. That was Hebrew he spoke."

"You are correct, Doctor Connor." It was the man who had shouted at Nick. He wore a yellow shirt.

"You were at Mount Nebo," Nick said.

"Yes. Someone would like to talk with you."

CHAPTER THIRTEEN

The van pulled into an abandoned factory on the southern edge of the city. Holes in the floor marked where machinery had been bolted down. Rusted barrels were stacked high in one corner. Light shone on scattered debris through gaping holes in the roof.

The man with the yellow shirt said, "This way."

"Who are you?" Nick said.

"Please, this way."

They followed him up a flight of metal steps into what had been the manager's office. Their footsteps echoed across the empty space. Broken windows looked out over the deserted factory floor. Inside the office was a battered metal desk with a man sitting behind it.

"Ari!" Nick said. "What the hell are you doing here?"

Ari Herzog was a senior operative in Shin Bet. Shin Bet was Israel's invisible shield, like the FBI and NSA combined, responsible for internal security and counter-terrorism. Nick knew him from Jerusalem, two years before.

Herzog stood. "Waiting for you, Nick. As usual, things are interesting around you." He reached out and clasped Nick's shoulder and shook his hand. "You look the same. It is good to see you, my friend."

"And you." He turned to Selena. "Selena, this is Ari Herzog. A friend from Israel."

"Nick told me about you."

"A pleasure, Doctor Connor. Please, sit," Herzog said.

Herzog wore a white shirt that looked comfortably worn. He wasn't wearing a tie. A dark blue jacket with wide lapels hung loose enough to reveal a shoulder holster and the butt of a Jericho 9mm pistol. He wore black pants and plain black shoes.

Herzog's eyes were dark, intense and tired looking, his face lined by stress and years of responsibility.

"It's good to see you too, Ari. Thanks for bailing us out back there. But why have you been following us? I spotted your man." He gestured at Yellow Shirt.

Herzog ignored the question. "That's Lev," he said. Lev had the grace to look embarrassed. "This is Aaron and Gabriel." He gestured at the other two. Gabriel had fired the grenade. They nodded. Both men had the look.

"You haven't answered my question, Ari. Why were you following us?"

"Because you are searching for the Ark." The words hung in the air between them. "We know about the death of the French bookseller and the manuscript."

Something clicked in Nick's mind. "You thought we might lead you to it."

Herzog nodded. "I was picked to contact you because we worked together before. I did not expect trouble so soon, but trouble seems to follow you." He smiled to show he was only half serious.

"Who came after us in the square?"

"Thugs hired to eliminate you. We suspected something might happen. Others are also looking for the Ark."

Nick's head felt as though someone had begun to tighten a band around it.

"I don't suppose you'd like to tell me who sent them?"

"We don't know for sure. The desk clerk tipped the gunmen off that you were leaving."

"Why come after us?"

"Someone doesn't want you to succeed. The Ark would boost Israel in the eyes of the world. "

Nick felt his blood pressure rising. A headache started. *He's not telling me something. What the hell is going on?*

"So you were letting us do the work for you and take the risks. Did you plan to let us in on this, Ari?"

Herzog looked down at his fingernails. When he looked up again, Nick saw he was now talking to Shin Bet and the Government of Israel. Ari might be a friend but his country came before friendship.

"What have you learned, Nick?"

"I think we'll call Director Harker," Selena said, "before we tell you anything."

Nick had been so focused on Herzog that he'd almost forgotten she was there. He looked at her.

"You didn't see fit to warn us that someone might come after us," she said to Herzog, "warn your *friend*." Herzog winced at the way she said it.

She turned to Nick. "We shouldn't tell him anything without talking to Elizabeth. Call her. Assuming we're not prisoners here."

Ari sighed. "You are not prisoners, Doctor Connor. Go ahead, Nick, call."

Nick's headache exploded behind his eyes. He rubbed his forehead.

"Are you all right?"

"I'm fine." He took out his phone and entered the code. Harker picked up after one ring.

"Yes, Nick."

"Director, we have a situation." He ran it down for her. When he finished, there was silence at the other end.

"Director?"

"I'm here." Nick heard her pen tapping in the background. "Tell Herzog that the file led you to Mount Nebo. Don't mention Mount Sinai or what we talked about earlier. I'm going to have to go to the President. You can't say anything else until I consult with the White House. There are international complications now that Israel is involved."

"You intend to follow up with him?" Nick asked.

"Pending the President's okay, yes."

"What if he wants the file?"

"Stall him. I don't want the Israelis to get it just yet. Tell him I will forward a copy to him. Now get home." She ended the call.

Nick looked at Ari.

"Director Harker is concerned about the political implications. She wants to consult with our President. I can tell you what we've got but the truth is we don't know where the Ark is hidden. She says she'll send you a copy of the manuscript and keep you in the loop."

"The Ark is not on Mount Nebo, everyone knows that. Why come here?"

Nick told him about the Nostradamus quatrain that had led to Mount Nebo. He didn't mention his idea about Moses and the Ten Commandments.

"What is the American expression?" Herzog said. "You might be on a wild duck chase?"

"Goose chase. Goose, not duck. If it's a wild goose chase, why are people trying to kill us?"

Herzog evaded the question. He looked at his watch. "You can still make your flight. Lev will drive you to the airport."

He got up. Nick and Selena stood.

"We need to go to our embassy first."

"I have your word you will keep me informed? If you catch a goose?"

"You do."

"That's good enough. Shalom, Nick."

Herzog watched Lev drive away with Nick and Selena.

"Why didn't you tell him about the Americans?" Gabriel said.

"Because we're not certain. His unit is good. If something is there, he'll find it."

"Why would he tell us if he did? He's not one of us."

"No," Ari said. "But he's a friend."

CHAPTER FOURTEEN

Harker had been to the White House many times in the last 5 years. She was used to the protocols but she'd never gotten used to the aura of power that enveloped the building. Secret Service agents met her at a side entrance, put her weapon in a locked cabinet and gave her a visitor's pass to hang around her neck. An agent escorted her to the Oval Office. She'd put on one of her good suits for the visit, the Prada.

The Rose Garden was in full bloom. President Rice stood looking out at the explosion of color. He turned when she entered. James Rice was in the first year of his second term. He still had a lot of political clout, but lame duck status was creeping up on him. There were days like today when he wished he had never seen the inside of the White House, much less the Oval Office.

Rice had served in Vietnam as a Marine Lieutenant. He was about six feet tall, not a particularly handsome man, but he radiated authority. He had charisma, that indefinable something that you knew when you saw it. Elizabeth thought he was probably the best President since Jefferson or Lincoln.

Rice watched Harker enter the Oval Office and suspected she was about to give him another problem about the Middle east. Everything about the Middle East was a nightmare. Iraq was slipping into civil war. He'd known it would all along, in spite of the feel good propaganda about democracy. The Saudis and OPEC were playing games with the oil supplies and speculators were driving prices up at the pump in pursuit of quick profits. Egypt was a powder keg. The Russians were making trouble about Syria. The last thing he needed were more problems in the region.

He said none of this to her.

"Elizabeth, how are you? I can give you ten minutes."

"Fine, Mister President, thank you."

They both sat down on a couch.

"Sir, there is a potential situation developing that involves Israel. Possibly Saudi Arabia as well."

"There is always a situation with those two. What is it this time?"

One of the reasons Elizabeth liked Rice was his no-nonsense approach to the job. He didn't avoid the issues. It was why he'd hired her to create and run the Project. To make sure he knew about issues before they blew up in his face.

"It involves the Ark of the Covenant."

"Religion."

"Yes, sir."

"It's always religion at the middle of everything over there. What about the Ark?"

Elizabeth briefed him about the Nostradamus file and the Ark. She told him about Herzog.

"What do you propose, Director?"

"Sir, I think we need to pursue this, in cooperation with the Israelis. If there's any possibility the Ark exists and can be located, we have to find it. We need to continue to search for it, but not until we have a better idea of where to look."

"What kind of cooperation with the Israelis?"

"Information only. I don't think they should be involved in any other way. The Ark is a very big deal for them. We don't need them interfering or overreacting and doing something that gets everyone in trouble. The best way to do that is feed them intelligence as seems suitable."

"If it becomes known that I sent covert operatives over there to look for a religious object, it will ignite a firestorm."

"Yes, sir, but I still think we should do it if we have good intel on the possible location."

Rice stood. Elizabeth rose with him. "I don't need to know details. If you mount an operation, don't get caught."

That's clear enough, she thought. *You're on your own.*

"Yes, Mister President. Thank you, sir."

"Better save the thanks for later," he said.

CHAPTER FIFTEEN

"I need a couple of days to go to California," Nick said. Elizabeth waited. "My mother is ill and she's probably not going to make it. There are things I have to take care of. Family stuff."

Nick's family consisted of his mother and his sister Shelley. Nick didn't get along with his sister and he never would, as best he could tell. They never had, not as kids, not now. He didn't want to make this trip, but he had to go.

"Get back as soon as you can. I need you here." Harker picked up her pen and set it down. "I'm sorry, Nick."

Nick nodded. "It's not unexpected. I'll go today."

When he'd left, Elizabeth leaned back in her chair and looked out at the flowers in the garden behind the house. No one would dream that millions of dollars worth of high end computers and hi-tech weaponry lay underneath.

She didn't miss the old building. Her old office didn't have windows or natural light. Here there was the garden to distract her when her mind got clogged with the endless, devious details of her job. Her father would have understood. The Judge had loved flowers. He'd spent hours cultivating his garden in the Colorado summer evenings. He'd loved to talk about the garden.

Flowers are a lot simpler to please than people. A little food, the right amount of water, good earth to grow in, a place in the sun and they're happy. Seems like humans ought to be able to learn something from that.

She smiled at the memory.

Her thoughts turned to the Ark. The whole thing was probably a dangerous waste of time. Her team would be going into harm's way looking for something that might not exist. And what if it did exist? What if they managed against all odds to find it? What then?

The Israelis would never tolerate possession of the Ark by anyone except themselves. Nor would the Muslims, either Sunni or Shia. All three groups would kill each other to obtain it and her team could get caught in the crossfire. At least there weren't any significant Christian powers in play to complicate things even more. Three great world religions, one common background and few people with a willingness to find unity in their mutual roots.

Not at all like flowers.

Finding the Ark would just be the beginning. It was a good thing it wasn't up to her to decide what would be done with it if they succeeded. That would fall on the President's shoulders. Elizabeth didn't envy him the responsibility.

She had enough of her own.

CHAPTER SIXTEEN

The hospice in Palo Alto was pleasant enough. It was better pleasant than not, when it came time to die. Nick had seen enough death in places that were anything but pleasant.

His mother had a private room. She lay in the bed, partly raised up. An oxygen tube fed whispers of life into her nostrils. Machines beeped and recorded the irregular beating of her heart. A hanging plastic bag fed clear liquid into her veins.

Something twisted inside as he looked at her.

The left side of her face was paralyzed and slack. Saliva drooled from the corner of her mouth. Her eyes were filmy and unfocused. Each labored breath was a shudder. Nick looked at the husk of what had once been a vibrant human being and thought about how life had betrayed her.

There hadn't been much joy in his mother's life. Not after she'd married his father, anyway. Nick's father had been a drunk, a womanizer and a bully. Sometimes Nick thought there should be a list for people like his father, labeled *terrorist, domestic*. But people like his father fell into a part of society that could get away with a form of terrorism because he was married. Being married put you in a different category. The culture of acceptance surrounding domestic violence was changing, Nick knew, but too late for him and his mother.

Nick had watched the light fade from his mother's eyes as he grew up, watched her endure beatings and humiliation. His father had done the same to him, until he was finally big enough and strong enough to fight back. That had happened when he was sixteen.

He remembered.

The punch sent his mother sprawling across the kitchen floor.

"Leave her alone!"

"Shut up, you little punk." His father started toward him. Nick's vision turned red, the first time the mist descended over his eyes. The next thing he remembered was his sister screaming and pulling on his arm with all her strength.

"Nick, stop! Stop! You're killing him! Please, stop!"

His arm was raised in the air, his fist clenched white. He was kneeling on his father's chest. His father was crying and pleading, trying to protect his head, his face covered with blood, his shirt bloody. Blood on the floor. Blood on Nick. He could feel drops of his father's blood on his face.

"Nick. Enough." His mother's voice, frightened, cutting through the red mist.

He looked down at his father and knew what hatred felt like. He lowered his fist.

His father had never touched his mother again.

"Mister Carter? Are you all right?"

The voice of the nurse shocked him back into the present. His fists were clenched tight, like they'd been that day.

"Yes, fine."

"Visiting hours are over."

"All right." He looked again at his mother. He reached out and touched her arm.

"Gotta go, Mom. I'll see you tomorrow."

There was no response. He hadn't expected any.

The next morning she was dead. Nick could feel that she was gone the moment he walked into the building. His sister Shelley and her husband were at the front desk talking with the head nurse.

"You're too late, Nick," she said. There was something in her voice, a quiet satisfaction, that set his anger coiling. "Somehow I'm not surprised."

"Now Shel," her husband said.

She turned on him. "Shut up, George," she said. "He's never been around when it mattered. Only when he was beating up on the man who put a roof over his head."

Nick stared at this person who was supposed to be part of his family. His head suddenly felt like someone had put it in a vise and cranked it shut. He wanted to choke her. With an effort, he controlled the urge.

"You are truly a first-class bitch," Nick said. "You can't let it go even on the day of our mother's death, can you? Daddy's little girl finally gets to balance the books."

"How dare you!" Shelley flushed pink.

The nurse stared at them open mouthed.

"Where is my mother?" Nick said to her.

"She's still in her room, Mister Carter. But I think..."

"I don't care what you think."

Nick pushed his sister out of the way and walked down to his mother's room. Someone had pulled the sheet over her face. He folded it back. Her cheeks had sunken in, all the tension had gone from her face. It wasn't peaceful, it was just the absence of anything. There was no one there. Whatever she had been was gone.

He sat down next to the bed and stared at the body. He wanted to say something. No, that wasn't right. He wanted to feel something, but all he felt was a kind of indifferent numbness.

I'm sorry, he thought.

Gently, he folded the sheet back over her. He walked back out to the entrance. Shelley and her husband were standing outside. She had always taken their father's side. She still did. Shelley had been daddy's girl. Carter senior had never gone after her, only Nick and his mom. Shelley had spent the last couple of years trying to get his mother moved into a home so she and her husband could get their hands on her house, but Nick had blocked her.

Rage at his sister welled up inside. He didn't trust himself to speak. He walked past her and got in his rental car and drove off. Arrangements for the funeral had been in place for months. There was nothing left to do, except go back to Washington.

He wasn't ready to go back to Washington.

Nick decided to drive up to his cabin property in the foothills. He hadn't been back since the night the cabin burned. He hadn't wanted to come back. For a while the place had been a refuge from the madness of his job. Then the madness had followed him there.

He came up the familiar gravel road and pulled in where he'd always parked. The blackened remains of the cabin rose from the weeds. He got out of the car and walked to where the porch had been. He heard something, a low noise. He listened. It came again, a plaintive meow.

A portion of decking had escaped the blaze, raised off the ground. Nick got on his knees and peered underneath the scorched planks. An orange shape lay underneath, just beyond the edge.

"Burps," he said.

He reached under the boards and laid his hand on the cat. The fur felt matted and stiff. Nick worked his hands underneath and gently slid him cat from under the ruined deck. Burps began to purr, a raspy, sputtery sound that was half his normal volume.

The thick orange fur was stiff with dried blood. There was a long gash along his hindquarters, a tear along his side.

Shit, Nick thought. "It's okay big guy, I've got you," he said. "You need a doctor. Come on."

He cradled the cat in his arms and stood. Burps had appeared one day out of the woods and adopted Nick and later, Selena. He came and went but always showed up whenever Nick came to the cabin.

He was a big cat but he'd lost a lot of weight. He kept purring as Nick carried him to the truck. Nick laid him on the seat and pulled a blanket out of the back of the cab. He put Burps on the blanket and folded it part way over him. He closed the door, got in the driver's side and headed back down

the hill. There was a vet not far away. That evening he called
Harker and told her he'd be delayed a few days.

CHAPTER SEVENTEEN

Selena held Burps in her lap. His hind leg was wrapped in a bandage. He purred and drooled on her jeans past his one front tooth.

"He's still weak," Nick said. "The vet said he'd probably been lying there for a few days without food or water. Might have been a dog that got him. It took 20 stitches to put him back together. He's full of antibiotics, too."

"He's getting old," she said. "It was only a matter of time before something caught him. What are we going to do with him? He can't stay here, he's a Tom. Once he recovers he won't be happy inside like this."

She was right. In California, Burps had been king of the woods around Nick's cabin. He'd lived in the open all his life.

"I couldn't leave him in California, he would have died. I was thinking he could live at the Project. Lots of room outside, mice to chase, a fence to keep the dogs away. Trees to climb, if he wants. Kind of a perfect cat retirement home, if you ask me. We owe him. It's why I brought him back East."

They did owe him. Burps had saved their lives one night. As if he knew what they were thinking, the cat looked up at Selena with half-open eyes and gave a loud, contented belch. It was why Nick had given him his name.

"That would work." She looked at him. "What's the matter? You've got that serious look you get sometimes."

"I've been thinking about what you said. About seeing someone. I made an appointment with a counselor for tomorrow afternoon."

"You did?" She was surprised. She hadn't thought he'd do it.

"He's on a list of people with security clearance. He specializes in PTSD and he was in Afghanistan. That's one reason I picked him. I couldn't talk to someone who hasn't been through it. They wouldn't understand."

As Selena petted the cat, she felt uncertainty twist in her gut. *Things are going to change. If he goes to the first appointment. If he keeps going.* She wanted him to go. Things couldn't go on like they had been, she was certain of that. But no one could predict what it would stir up.

She'd have to wait and see.

CHAPTER EIGHTEEN

A spiral staircase behind a three inch steel door led down into the Project operations center. Except for the lack of windows and the absence of external noises, the room could have been anywhere in the normal world. The walls were painted a light peach color. Soothing landscapes hung on the walls, Selena's doing. The ceiling was high and light, painted off white. The room felt comfortable and spacious. In essence, it was a luxury cave.

Nick, Ronnie, Selena, Lamont and Stephanie sat at a table facing a wall monitor displaying a large map of Saudi Arabia. Stephanie had a keyboard and laptop in front of her, linked to the Crays in the other room.

North of Saudi Arabia lay Iraq and Kuwait. The northwest was bordered by Jordan and the tip of Israel. West was the Sinai Peninsula and Egypt. South was Yemen. After Yemen came Oman, Qatar, Bahrain and the United Arab Emirates. On the west lay the Red Sea and on the east, the Persian Gulf. Iran was not far away.

Nothing but trouble, Nick thought.

"Here's the problem," he said. "All we've got is speculation and guesses. People have been looking for the Ark for a long time. Some of them looked in Saudi Arabia and no one's ever found anything that matters. We can pick a volcano, but we might as well throw darts at the map. It's a waste of time without knowing more. Any ideas how we should proceed?"

"If we knew the route Moses took, we might be able to pin down the mountain where he got the Commandments," Ronnie said.

"You're assuming the story in Exodus is true, or at least based on facts."

"We have to start somewhere."

Selena said, "No one knows the route, just that the Exodus started in Egypt. The Israelites head east and God parts the waters of the Red Sea."

"How come this mountain is supposed to be in the Sinai?" Lamont asked. "They wouldn't need to cross the Red Sea to go there."

"Depends on where they started from," Selena said. "If they started in the south of Egypt, they might have crossed it. It's possible they started from an area northeast of modern Cairo. If that's true, they wouldn't need to cross the water. The story about the Red Sea could be just that, a story to illustrate God's power and protection."

"You know," Nick said, "the more I look at this map, the less I buy the idea the Ark is in Saudi Arabia. Put yourself in Moses' shoes."

"Moses didn't wear shoes," Lamont said. "He wore sandals."

Selena rolled her eyes. "What are you thinking, Nick?"

"Moses had thousands of people following him. Women, kids, animals, whatever they could carry."

"Go on."

"If you're Moses, you want to get out of Egypt as quickly as possible. Look at the map. What's the best route?"

"East," Ronnie said. "Due east."

"Right. So the Israelites head east. If they start north of Cairo they don't need to cross the Red Sea. There were trade routes back then, people knew where things were and they knew how to get from one place to another without getting lost. There's no reason for Moses to enter what's now Saudi Arabia. That means Mount Sinai can't be an Arabian volcano. Selena, where's the traditional location?"

"In the south of the Sinai Peninsula, near the tip."

"Why would they go there?" Ronnie asked. "That's completely out of the way. It doesn't make sense."

"Forty years wandering in the desert, right? Isn't that what happened?" Lamont said.

"The forty years was after Moses went up the mountain," Selena said.

"We're getting off the track," Nick said.

Selena took a sip of water from a bottle. "It would make sense to follow one of the trade routes from Egypt. That way there would be known quantities, like water and shelter, firewood, things like that."

"I can show the routes," Stephanie said. "Give me a minute."

She entered a few keystrokes. Colored lines in purple, green and black appeared on the map.

"Those are the main routes at the time of Moses. The top line is called the Way of the Philistines," she said. "The Bible says they didn't go that way."

"Take it out," Nick said. "If we're going to use the Bible as a guide we have to be consistent."

She entered a command and the purple line disappeared. That left the green line and the black one. The black line wandered down the western edge of the Sinai peninsula to Mount Sinai and up again, until it crossed the third route in green.

"We've already decided the traditional Mount Sinai isn't going to give us much. Let's go with the idea Moses took the shortest way," Nick said. "If that's right, then we can take out the black line and the traditional mountain. Go ahead, Steph."

She moved her mouse, clicked. The black line disappeared.

"The green route heads into Jordan," Stephanie said.

"Are there any volcanoes on that route?"

"Doesn't look like it." Stephanie pressed keys. "Nope."

"Dead end," Lamont said.

"All right." Nick rubbed his forehead. He had another headache coming on. "We're not going to Jordan or anywhere else without better intel."

He looked at his watch. His first counseling appointment was that afternoon.

"Everyone go home, clear your head. I'll tell Harker where we're at. Steph, see if you can find anything on that green route that matches the biblical story. Meet back here at 0800 tomorrow."

Nick rode back with Selena to D.C. Her Mercedes still had that new car smell of leather and wax. Better than the smell of the car was a hint of the perfume Selena wore.

"What's that scent you're wearing?"

"You like it?" She smiled. He loved it when she smiled. "It's called *Baccart Les Larmes Sacrees de Thebe.*"

"That's a mouthful."

"It's supposed to invoke the mystery of ancient Egypt. The perfume comes in a bottle of Baccarat crystal."

"That's good?"

"Very good."

Nick had been glancing in his side mirror. He sighed.

"Not again."

"What, not again?"

"We're being followed. Silver Lexus, four cars back."

She looked in her mirror. "I see him."

"Two men. He's keeping his distance."

"I can lose him."

"Not yet. We don't need another shootout on the Beltway. Be ready in case he speeds up."

"You're sure he's following us."

They were coming up on Alexandria. "Let's find out. Take the next exit."

The Lexus followed them off 495 into Alexandria. Selena cruised up South Henry Street.

"Head for the waterfront," Nick said.

She turned right. The Lexus was still behind them. It had dropped back a block, trying to stay unnoticed. Signs pointed to Founder's Park.

"Park over there in the lot. Let's take a little walk."

She slipped the Mercedes into a spot. They got out and began walking. The path forked around a stand of trees in full leaf. The gray-blue waters of the Potomac were visible beyond the trees, wide and calm.

He thought of the story about George Washington and the Potomac. He looked at the river. *No way Washington threw that silver dollar across.*

The day was warm, the air filled with the scent of fresh cut grass and the damp smell of the river. Clusters of people strolled about, enjoying the fine weather. A group of sullen teenagers passed them. The boys gave Selena lewd looks. Nick smelled marijuana as they went by.

The men from the car had followed them into the park. Nick felt a light sweat starting. He wanted to take off his jacket but he didn't want to upset the citizens. Shoulder holsters and guns tended to do that.

The path they were on led to a long pier that angled left and then straight ahead. A river tour boat was docked at the end, getting ready to sail. Passengers were going through a caged ticketing area. Nick headed for the pier as if they planned to board.

"Want to take a boat ride?"

"You'll miss your appointment."

"Spoilsport. All right, let's see what they'll do if we turn around."

They did an about face and walked toward the two men. Both men had short hair and looked as if they worked out a lot. Their expressions were unfriendly. They both wore jackets. One man was taller than the other. He needed a shave and he wore a blue sport coat. He reached inside his jacket.

Everything after that was instinct.

As the gun came out, Nick gave off a piercing shout he'd learned from Selena. It froze Blue Coat in the act of raising his pistol for a split fraction of time, long enough. Nick got his pistol free and fired at the center of Blue Coat's body. He missed and fired again and watched blood blossom on the shirt. Blue Coat staggered backward and fell. Chaos and screams erupted in the park. Panicked people scrambled to get out of the way.

The second man pulled his jacket away with his left hand, exposing a MAC-10. He fired a one-handed burst as Nick swung toward him. Someone cried out on the pier. Selena shot him before he could get off another burst. She shot him again. He doubled over and fell to his knees. He tried to lift the gun. Nick and Selena fired at the same time. The man fell to his side. He twitched and stopped moving.

They walked over and kicked the guns away from the bodies. Both men were dead. Nick holstered his gun.

"I hate this," he said.

"Better call your therapist," she said. "You're going to be late."

Nick looked down at the bodies. "Gives me something to talk about."

"That's not funny," she said.

"No," he said, "it isn't."

CHAPTER NINETEEN

"No IDs on the two in the park," Harker said. "The car is a rental. The license and credit card they used are fakes. Good fakes, I might add. I wish you hadn't killed them."

"We didn't have a choice."

"I had to call in some serious pressure to get you out of there. I'm not sure it's over yet. Everyone is nervous about guns going off in public places. The spin is that those two were terrorists and you were Federal Agents. Some people think you're heroes. Some people want to make an example of you."

"Are we subject to political correctness now? Those two called the play."

"I know. I'll take care of it. The real question is who were they and why did they go after you."

"They picked us up on the Beltway," Nick said. "They had to know we were coming from here."

"So much for our new anonymity. I guess it was just wishful thinking." She picked up her Mont Blanc. "The quality of the fake IDs indicates pros. We're running the prints to see if anything turns up."

"It has to be about the Ark," Selena said. "The same people who sent gunmen after us in Jordan."

"Someone who has a lot of resources," Nick said. "Serious connections and serious money. You don't just hire a truck or two full of guys with automatic weapons by walking into the local rent-a-terrorist agency. Like you said, pros."

"I don't understand why they keep trying to kill you. Wouldn't it make more sense to grab you, find out what you know?" Harker turned her pen around in her fingers.

"Maybe they already know what we know. Or they know where the Ark is and don't want us to find it."

"Are you any closer to pinpointing a location?"

"Only by elimination. No matter what we decide, we'll still be guessing. We'd get better odds in Vegas."

"Give it your best shot, Nick. We can't let it drop. Things have gone too far."

CHAPTER TWENTY

Counseling.

The word was uncomfortable. In Nick's mind, going to a shrink meant you'd failed. It meant there was something you couldn't handle on your own. He'd been handling things on his own as long as he could remember. He'd told Selena that and she'd said maybe that was the problem. It had made him angry.

It was because he'd struck out at Selena in his sleep that he was here in this office. That, and the fact that whenever he thought about his mother he felt nothing. Wasn't he supposed to feel something? It was as if he'd buried the feelings somewhere and forgotten where he put them. All he felt when he thought about her was guilty for not feeling more.

He was having the Afghanistan nightmare every night. He was tired. Tired meant he could make a mistake that would get someone killed. He felt stretched out like a high, tight wire over a bottomless pit. If counseling could make the dreams go away, it was worth the confrontation with his pride.

The waiting area was quiet. The carpet was wall to wall, a soft gray under foot. He sat on one of the chairs and tapped his fingers on his knee. The furniture was comfortable. A copy of a Paul Klee painting hung on one wall. Nick liked Klee. Seeing the picture there helped. Someone who liked Klee couldn't be all bad. Maybe it would be okay.

The door to the inner office opened. The man standing there was older than Nick by a few years. He wore khaki slacks, comfortable brown shoes and a checked shirt open at the collar. He'd been Special Forces and came recommended. He was about Nick's height and a little heavier. His left sleeve was pinned up against his shoulder.

"Nick? I'm Dave Milton. Come on in."

They shook hands. Milton gestured to a chair. "Have a seat."

"Do I call you Doctor or what?"

"Doctor is fine. Doc, if you prefer." He sat down in a wingback chair a few feet away. Nick looked around. A half dozen diplomas, an Army discharge certificate and several award plaques hung on the walls.

"Let me guess," Milton said. "Marines?"

"Recon. Thirteen years."

Milton nodded. "How did you hear about me?"

"A guy I know from Afghanistan."

Milton nodded.

Nick said, "I have to tell you. I'm not sure this is going to help anything."

"It might not."

"Aren't you supposed to tell me it will?"

"Would you believe me if I did?"

"Probably not."

"There you go."

Milton looked relaxed. His presence was calming. *Probably a good thing in a shrink*, Nick thought.

"How does this work?" he said.

"You come in. We talk about whatever you want to talk about. Everything is confidential."

"That's all?"

"What did you expect?"

"I don't know. Maybe some tests. Questions about my childhood, that kind of thing."

"Nope. Just conversation."

"What if I just want to talk about football?"

Milton shrugged. "It's your money. You might get better results if you talk about what's bugging you."

"I can't talk about what I do."

"If it's important, you'll find a way to talk about it. Where do you want to begin?"

"What happened to the arm?" Nick said.

"Afghanistan happened. You were there?"

"I was." Nick thought about how he'd hit Selena in his sleep. "I have this dream," he said. "I'm back in Afghanistan, on a mission that went bad."

After he'd described the dream, Nick waited.

"Is that what happened on the mission?" Milton asked.

"Pretty much."

"Was there anything else you could have done?"

"I don't know."

"Think back. You were taking heavy fire."

"Yeah. Then this kid comes out of the doorway."

"And you hesitated."

"He was a kid."

"With a grenade."

Nick was silent.

"Where was the rest of your unit?"

"Taking fire. There must have been twenty Tallies on the roof. My sergeant was down, three of the others."

"How many died?" Milton asked.

"What do you mean?"

"How many of your men died?"

"What's that got to do with it?"

"How do you feel about the men that died?"

"How do you think I feel?"

"I don't know unless you tell me. Do you feel responsible?"

Rage.

Nick stood. "Fuck you."

He walked out.

CHAPTER TWENTY-ONE

"Are you going to tell me how it went?" Selena said. It was late in the afternoon. Nick was making coffee. They were in his apartment.

"You mean the counseling thing?"

"You haven't said anything about it."

"There isn't much to say."

"What happened?"

"I told him about the dream. He wanted to know how I felt about what happened."

"And?"

"I don't want to talk about it. You want coffee?"

"You're changing the subject. Yes, I want coffee. Why don't you want to talk about it? That's the whole point. Talking about it."

"I've talked to you."

"I'm not a therapist."

"I don't see the point. Talking won't change anything." He brought her a cup. "That kid is still dead. So are my men."

"That's not your fault."

"Damn it!" He slammed his cup down on the table. She jumped. Coffee slopped out over the clean surface. "It is my fault. I was in command. So stop with the platitudes."

Selena looked at him. "You walked out, didn't you? You didn't finish the session."

He was silent.

"You need to go back. For yourself. For us. I can't keep dealing with this."

She was wearing a long sleeved blouse. Selena pulled it up along her ribs. Her side was turning black and blue.

"That's from last night. You didn't even wake up. You yelled something and started thrashing around."

He stared at the bruise. "I did that?"

"Now do you see why you have to go back?"

He sat down, let out a long breath.

"I'll think about it."

Selena got up. "You do that. You think about it."

She walked to the door.

"Where are you going?"

"Home. While you think about it." The door slammed behind her. Her untouched coffee steamed on the table. He stared at the door. It had nothing to say.

He decided to go for a run. Running helped him clear his mind. Nothing to think about except the feel of the pavement under his feet and the movement of his body. He changed into sweats and put on his running shoes. He tucked a Colt .380 under his sweatshirt and took the elevator down. He stepped out of the entrance and saw a black, armored limousine waiting by the curb.

Adam, he thought. *Damn.*

Adam was an unknown quantity. Every time he showed up things got difficult. It always meant trouble.

The driver held the rear door open. Nick wondered how Adam managed to time his arrivals to catch him when he was coming out of his building. He got in the car. The door closed and he heard the click of the lock going home.

The car was a Cadillac Presidential Model, several hundred thousand dollars worth of armored protection and luxury. The protection part was handled by run flat tires, 5 inches of armor plate, a turbo charged engine with over 500 horses, bullet proof glass and for all Nick knew, rocket launchers. The seats were covered in smooth black leather. The carpet was dark blue. The windows were completely blacked out. Halo lighting on the padded roof cast a soft glow over the interior.

The driver was invisible behind a partition of black glass. A floor to ceiling panel of black glass divided the entire rear compartment straight down the middle, making it impossible to see who or what was on the other side. There was a speaker grill at head height in the partition and a slot where things could be passed back and forth.

"Hello, Nick."

The voice was masked with electronics, as if it were underwater. The sound was eerie in the confined space of the car.

"Adam."

The car began moving.

"You've stepped into a hornet's nest again. How do you manage it?"

"Just lucky, I guess. What's going on, Adam?"

"You have become a problem for some very powerful people. Have you heard of Cask and Swords?"

"No."

"Cask and Swords is a network of men prominent in every important aspect of American government, finance and business. That includes the military and the Pentagon. Members are recruited during their junior year at the University and sworn to lifelong secrecy. Money, intelligence and connections are required for consideration. There are no female members, no minorities, no Jews."

"A conspiracy, you mean?"

"They would not call it that. If they were to talk about it at all, they would probably say that they share a natural consensus about what the world needs to further their aims. They would couch it in terms of national security and the best policies for the nation."

"What are their aims?"

"Power, wealth and control. There's nothing new about that. That's the way it's always been. What's new is that a small, hard core faction has decided that America needs another war."

"They never quit, do they?"

"No. That's where you come in. You got involved when Bertrand sent you the Nostradamus manuscript."

It didn't surprise Nick that Adam knew about the manuscript.

The electronic voice continued. "The Ark is the symbol of God's agreement with the human race and the guarantor of Israel's legitimacy. It can be used to provoke a war."

"It probably doesn't even exist."

"The men behind this think it does. They're looking for it. That's why those gunmen came after you in Jordan and Virginia. They don't want you interfering in their plans and they don't want you to find it."

"Something doesn't make sense. We're the ones who have the manuscript. Why would they want to take us out without finding out what's in it?"

"Because they already know what's in it. Yours isn't the only copy. Bertrand was paranoid. He made a copy and sent it to himself."

"His place in Provence?"

"Yes. Cask and Swords found it."

"But no one has the Ark. I don't understand how that fits with what you say is their goal. Starting a war."

"If they can find it, they'll use it to raise tensions in the Middle East to the breaking point. War would follow. The US would get involved. Cask and Swords members behind this would make a great deal of money. There is also a religious component. One of the leaders is somewhat fanatical. He wants to instigate a new crusade against Islam."

The car stopped. After a moment it began moving again. It was very quiet.

"What if there isn't any Ark?"

"Then they'll manufacture some provocation. These people already have great wealth. It's not just about the money, it's as much a game of power as anything else for them. They are determined to have their war. Just like before."

"Jesus, Adam."

"Follow the trail, Nick. Find it before they do. Watch your back. I'll help if I can."

The car came to a stop. Nick heard the lock click. After a moment the door was opened by the driver. Nick got out of the car. They were back in front of his building.

He watched the Cadillac pull away. He knew the license plate would yield no information. One day, he'd find out who Adam was. Right now that was the least of his concerns.

Watch your back.

CHAPTER TWENTY-ONE

Selena sat across from Nick in the Ops Center. She'd said nothing to him when he came in. Stephanie brought up a detailed map of Jordan on the monitor.

"In my opinion, the best place to look is Petra." She pointed at a spot on the map in the southern part of Jordan, 80 miles inland from the Israeli border.

"Why Petra?" Nick said.

"Look at the route we decided Moses had to take. It goes right to Petra."

The line was almost a straight shot from Egypt across to Jordan. At Petra it turned north to the Biblical Holy Land.

"There wasn't anything in Petra in the time of Moses," Lamont said. "Why go there?"

"There's a mountain there called Jabal al-Madhbaḥ. It's where Moses made water spring from a rock and where his brother Aaron is supposed to be buried. Sometimes winter storms in the area create vivid plasma displays. That could fit the description of fire on the mountain in the Bible."

"I don't know," Nick said, "that's slim."

"There's more. Petra is at the end of a narrow gorge. The wind comes through it and makes a trumpeting sound. The locals call it the Trumpet of God. That fits with the Bible story too."

"That's the place in the Indiana Jones movie," Lamont said. "The one about the Nazis and the Grail. Buildings carved out of red rock."

"I've been there," Selena said. "It's an amazing place."

"Tourists have been crawling over that place for years. There's no way the Ark is there." Nick shook his head.

"Remember the fourth quatrain?" Selena said.

Where water is bartered as gold
A small castle guards treasure beyond price
A cross and dome point the way
Beware the Red Horseman

"Go on."

She looked at him. Her voice was impersonal. "The people who lived there controlled the trade route. They built cisterns and canals to store water and sold it to travelers in the desert."

"Water bartered as gold."

"Yes. Petra is famous because of elaborate tombs carved out of red sandstone. When the sun hits it just right, the whole place turns red."

"Like Sedona," Ronnie said, "in Arizona."

Lamont started humming an Eagles tune.

"Any castles?" Nick asked.

"There's a crusader castle," Selena said, "in ruins."

"We could fly into Amman and play tourist," Lamont said.

Nick said, "Let me run it by Harker."

Upstairs he took Selena aside. "You're right. I'll make another appointment with the shrink."

"Why did you walk out of the last one?"

"I got angry. It felt like he was accusing me. But when I play it out in my mind, I can see that he wasn't."

"Are you going to tell him that?"

"I guess."

"Want to go get lunch somewhere?" she said.

CHAPTER TWENTY-TWO

"You pissed me off," Nick said.

Milton nodded.

"It sounded like you were blaming me for what happened. For the deaths."

"Why don't you talk about that?"

"You were there. You know what it's like."

"Yes. But we're not talking about me."

"Why is this important?"

"You tell me." Milton sipped from a mug with an inscription that read *I Used To Be Schizophrenic But We're So Much Better Now.*

"You're not going to give me much, are you?"

"What do you think I should give you?"

"I don't know. Advice, maybe? About how to stop the dream?"

"Would it help if we spent time analyzing it to try and figure out what it meant?"

"No. I already know what it means."

"There you go. Talk about that."

"Seems pretty straightforward. I had to kill a kid. I didn't want to. I feel bad about it."

"So why do you keep having the dream?"

"Isn't that what happens with PTSD? You have nightmares."

"More happened than just that kid. You were almost killed. Several of your men were killed."

"It's what happens in war."

"That's like saying the sky is blue."

Nick felt himself getting angry again.

"You're getting angry. Want to tell me why?"

"It feels like you're not listening. I say something and you throw another question at me or dismiss what I say."

"Because I said that about the sky."

"Yes."

"When you say people getting killed is what happens in war you're ducking the issue."

"What issue?"

"You tell me."

Nick wanted to get up and walk out again. He thought about Selena.

"I guess almost getting killed."

Milton nodded. It could have been approval. Or not. "How did you feel when you saw that grenade coming at you?"

Nick's back began hurting. "I didn't feel anything."

Milton waited. Nick remembered.

The boy's head explodes in a cloud of blood and bone. The grenade is in the air, coming at him. He starts to move but he can't get out of the way. He's helpless...

"I don't remember," Nick said.

Milton waited.

"Helpless," Nick said. Milton nodded, just a little.

"We're almost out of time," he said. "Do you want to come next week?"

"I'm going out of town. I'll have to call when I get back."

"Good," Milton said.

As Nick walked to his car he felt like something had happened, but he wasn't sure what it was.

CHAPTER TWENTY-THREE

They flew into Amman, rented a Land Rover and dropped Lamont and Selena at the hotel. From there Nick and Ronnie drove to the American Embassy. Harker had sent their weapons ahead in a diplomatic pouch.

The embassy didn't look like a diplomatic outpost. It looked like a fortress. It was a massive, white building three stories high, set back behind a high wall of fitted stone. An armored personnel carrier manned by Jordanian troops patrolled outside the wall. Palm trees planted at regular intervals tried and failed to create the impression of a normal building. A forest of antennas and satellite dishes rose from the roof. The windows were square and featured diamond shapes that reinforced the thick glass. Tall black iron fencing and metal gates blocked the entrances.

At the front desk they were directed to a room on the second floor. A brass nameplate on the door announced the office of Eric Anderson, Second Cultural Attaché.

"Agency," Ronnie said.

"Our man in Havana."

"Havana?"

"An old British movie about spies. It's a comedy," Nick said.

"I know you like those old movies," Ronnie said, "but these guys aren't very funny."

They knocked and went in. A blond man in his thirties sat behind a desk. He rose when they entered. He had the look of an athlete who was starting to go to seed. Nick's ear tingled.

"Carter?" Anderson said. "Been expecting you."

He smiled and held out his hand. Nick shook it.

"You have our package?" Nick asked.

"Yes. You do realize that Jordan is off limits for covert activity?"

"Who said anything about covert activity? We're here on vacation."

Anderson laughed. "Of course, sorry." He took a card from a case in his pocket and handed it to Nick. "You need anything while you're here, let me know. I'll call down about the package. Sign here."

He pushed a form across his desk. Nick signed it.

"Thanks. Appreciate it."

As they went down the stairs, Ronnie said, "I don't trust that guy."

"Me neither. But he doesn't concern us."

In the office they'd just left, Anderson was speaking on his private satellite phone with Phillip Harrison.

"They're here," he said. "I've talked with our friend. He's waiting for me to give him the heads up."

"Excellent."

Anderson wasn't worried about the call being intercepted. The phone he was using was encrypted with the latest technology. Only the chip at the other end could decode the transmission. The idea that all satellite transmissions could be successfully monitored was fiction. Captured, yes. Decrypted, no. Still, he spoke carefully out of habit.

"Do you want me to ask our friend to invite them to his house? They'd have a lot to talk about."

"It won't be necessary."

"I know he would like to entertain them."

"Entertainment has already been arranged." Harrison ended the call.

Anderson put his phone away and smiled.

CHAPTER TWENTY-FOUR

"We have to ride horses?" Lamont said.

"Where's your sense of adventure? No vehicles allowed. See the signs?" Nick pointed. "We can walk, or we can rent a horse. This looks like a good time for my hat."

"What hat?" Selena said.

Nick pulled out a crumpled brown felt hat and put it on. He tugged on the brim.

"You have got to be kidding," she said.

They stood outside the visitor center near the *Siq*, a narrow canyon that formed the entrance to Petra. They'd paid their fees and been provided with a mandatory guide. His name, he told them in passable English, was Ahmed.

Ahmed was short and dark, weathered from the sun. He grinned, flashing a metal tooth. "Horse better. You are friend of Indiana Jones, yes?"

"Yes. Okay, horses. Saddle up."

They took the horses at a walk though the narrow passage. The bottom of the Siq was deep in shadow. Higher up, the sun found the walls and turned them into glowing rose. The stone was alive with color, polished by millennia of sun and wind and water, marked with infinite striations of light and dark.

"This is really something," Ronnie said.

"Wait till you see the city," Selena said. "We're going to come out in front of what's called the Treasury. That's where they filmed the movie."

"When were you here?" Nick asked.

"My uncle brought me here when I was seventeen." Something passed over her face and was gone. "A lifetime ago."

Twenty minutes later they emerged from the *Siq*. The walls opened out and they were looking at the building called the Treasury.

"Wow," Lamont said.

The tomb was hewn from the rock of the canyon wall. The facade was a hundred and fifty feet high, carved with figures and faces. Six graceful columns with floral capstones rose to an elaborate, carved pediment. A wide flight of steps led to a porch cut into the mountain and the open entrance into the tomb. The interior of the tomb was in darkness. Above the pediment, the facade climbed up the side of the canyon and into the sun. Four more columns were topped by triangular pediments, placed to the sides of a central round tower capped with scalloped edges. Everything radiated a vibrant rose color in the sunlight.

"It's a big city," Selena said. "There are a lot of fancy tombs. But this one is special."

They dismounted.

Ahmed pointed at a group of donkeys tied nearby. "Horses no good, here. You ride or walk?"

"Walk," Nick said. "Ahmed, where is Jabal al-Madhbaḥ?"

"It is in front of you." The guide gestured at the tomb and the mountain above. "Very holy mountain."

"Can we walk to the top?"

"Yes, many steps. I show you."

They followed him to where the steps began.

"We'd like to go alone," Nick said. He slipped a 50 dinar note into Ahmed's hand, about $35.00 US.

Ahmed looked at the steps and the note disappeared into the folds of his gown.

"You must be very careful," he said. "Do not touch the altars."

"We'll be careful. Wait here for us."

Nick led the way. The steps were steep, cut from the rock wall. They were sweating by the time they reached the summit. Dozens of flat stone altars covered the top of the mountain.

"Gives me the creeps," Lamont said. "They must have done sacrifices here."

"Animals, not people," Selena said.

"Still gives me the creeps."

"Look for a cross and dome," Nick said. He took off his hat and wiped sweat away. "Isn't that what Nostradamus said?"

"It would be cut into the rock." Selena touched one of the altars. "It could be hard to see, worn by weather."

For an hour they examined the altars. They found nothing.

"There's nothing here," Ronnie said. "Just old rock."

"All right. We'll go back down and cool off."

Ahmed waited at the bottom of the steps. They walked over to the porch of the Treasury and sat on the top steps in the shade.

"You have enjoyed the view?" the guide said.

"Yeah, it was great." Lamont sat down with his back against a column.

"There's something else we should see," Selena said. Ahmed looked expectant. "There's a crusader castle here."

"Oh yes, two castles," Ahmed said.

"Two?"

"One very high on Jebal al Habis. You can only go so far. One smaller, very nice."

"A small castle," Nick said. He thought of the quatrain.

A small castle guards treasure beyond price.

"Show us the small one, Ahmed."

"We must walk through the city," he said. "Perhaps you would like something to drink? There is a stand not far away. My uncle runs it."

They bought cans of soda at the stand and walked past more of the impressive carved tombs. The castle was set off from the main part of the city, in a barren area. Ahmed guided them over rocky ground until they came to the building. It wasn't really a castle. It was an outpost of the larger Crusader ruin on top of the mountain.

Ahmed gave them the history. The fort had been built in the twelfth century and manned by fewer than a dozen men. Turkish soldiers had disguised themselves as villagers and surprised the Crusader knights as they came out of the chapel. All had been put to the sword. Ahmed seemed to take particular delight as he described the ambush and slaughter.

The fort was in good shape, considering. The walls still stood. The roof was gone. They climbed over rubble and entered what had been the chapel.

Selena stepped around the fallen stones. She came to a stop and stood looking at one of the walls. Nick joined her. Carved on the wall was a faint cross. Next to it was a faded, dome-like shape.

"The cross and the dome," she said. "That's a Templar cross. Those are Templar symbols."

"The Knights Templar?"

"The dome was a symbol for the Dome of the Rock in Jerusalem, or possibly the Church of the Holy Sepulcher. It was used on the Templar seal, along with two knights riding on one horse."

"Why only one horse?"

"It was a symbol of poverty."

Ronnie and Lamont came over. They heard what Selena said.

"The Templars weren't poor," Ronnie said. "They had lands, money, gold. Everyone knows that."

"They didn't start out that way." Selena peered at the wall.

"No one ever found their treasure, though," Lamont said.

"There's something else here," she said. "You can just make it out." She still had some soda in the can. Now she splashed it on the wall. Letters appeared under the cross, so faint that no one would likely notice them.

La maison de cinq arbres

"It's French."

"What does it mean?"

"The house of five trees."

"Five trees, again."

"We were wrong," she said. "The quatrain wasn't about the mountain where Moses got the Commandments. It was about this fort and this inscription. Nostradamus is pointing us at the Templars. We need to get back to the hotel and my computer."

"What have Templars got to do with the Ark?" Ronnie asked.

"They occupied Jerusalem during the Crusades. The Dome of the Rock was their headquarters. There are legends that the Ark was hidden in a secret chamber under the Temple Mount, and that the Templars took it with them when Jerusalem fell."

"The Templars." Nick shook his head. "Now it's the Templars as well as the Ark. Why is nothing ever simple?"

"Where's Ahmed?" Ronnie said.

"Probably taking a leak," Lamont said. "Here he comes." The guide came out from behind some rocks. He was putting a cell phone away.

"You wish to see the other castle?" Ahmed said.

"No. We're done."

"Then there is a shorter way to the visitor center."

Nick's ear began itching.

CHAPTER TWENTY-FIVE

It was late in the afternoon when they arrived back at the Visitor Center. The parking lot was almost empty. Nick gave Ahmed another 50 Dinar note. The guide seemed nervous. He thanked them and scurried away.

They walked over to the Land Rover. Nick's ear began to itch and burn. He pulled on it, hard.

"Oh, oh," Ronnie said.

"Something's wrong," Nick said.

They looked around. Everything seemed normal.

"There goes Ahmed."

Selena pointed at a white pickup speeding out of the lot. The guide was in the passenger seat. He didn't look back at them. The truck drove away fast, trailing plumes of dust.

"Kind of in a hurry," Lamont said.

"Remember when we were in Kabul?" Nick said to Ronnie. "That IED?"

"Yeah."

"I had the same sensation then."

"I don't see anything," Lamont said.

There was nothing in the area, no garbage bags, trash cans, packs, boxes, nothing that would conceal a threat. The nearest car was parked some distance away.

Lamont got down on his knees and peered under their truck. A black, oblong shape was stuck under the driver's side. A digital counter was marking down seconds in red. Lamont watched the numbers move past 20 to 19 to 18.

"Bomb!" he yelled. He scrambled to his feet. They ran.

They were more than a hundred feet away when the bomb detonated. The force of the blast knocked them to the dirt. Nick went sprawling. Pain jolted his spine. Chunks and pieces of the Land Rover fell around them. The hood crashed down into the parking lot ten feet from his head. All that remained of the truck was a jagged tangle of metal that burned with bright, hot light, sending a dense column of black smoke spiraling into the clear afternoon sky.

Nick got to his feet. He looked at the burning wreckage. Lamont came over to him.

"Smells like Semtex."

"Ahmed," Nick said. "Our friendly guide."

"Maybe you should have tipped him more," Lamont said.

CHAPTER TWENTY-SIX

The sat phone connection was good. "Everyone is all right?" Harker asked.

"Yes."

"No trouble about the guns?"

"No. The Jordanian cops are treating it as a terrorist attack on Western tourists. They never searched us. Selena distracted them. They even gave us a ride back to the hotel."

He shifted in the chair. His back was locked up tight.

"I'd like to get my hands on that guide. The bad guys just upped the ante."

"What's your plan now?" The connection sounded clear but far away.

"Selena is in the other room on the computer looking for something that ties into that inscription we found. We need to know where to go next. The inscription is the only lead we've got. If there's something there, she'll figure it out."

"I've been looking at Cask and Swords," Harker said. "Getting a membership list was next to impossible. People in this group are a who's who of American power. If they're behind this, we have a problem."

"We always have a problem."

"What I don't know is who is part of the core group Adam warned you about. There are a lot of people who would profit if there was another war. I'm working on narrowing down the list."

She paused. Nick heard her pen tapping in the background.

"There are several members who advise President Rice."

"You think Rice is involved?"

"No, I don't. He's not a member and everything he's done points the other way. But some of the people around him are. The Secretary of the Treasury, for example."

"Are you going to tell Rice about this?"

"Not until we have something concrete. I can't go to the President on the basis of what Adam told you. We don't even know who Adam is."

"You have a lot of credibility with Rice."

"Not that much. Follow up on what Selena finds out. Keep me up to date."

In Virginia, Elizabeth put down the phone. She looked through the bullet proof windows at the flowers growing over the underground rooms. The day was clear, sunny. She could have been in an average home almost anywhere in America. Project headquarters was anything but your average American home.

She looked at the list she'd compiled of Cask and Swords members. Who were the conspirators? She had no reason to doubt what Adam had told Nick. He'd been right in the past. His intel had prevented millions of deaths and probable war.

Elizabeth glanced at the picture of her father on the desk. She remembered a conversation with him from when she was fifteen. She'd had a complicated school science project due by the end of the week and hadn't been sure what would make it work. Her father had been in his usual chair, the big green one near the fireplace. It was a warm spring on the Western slope of the Rockies. The fire wasn't lit. The bourbon in his glass was warmth enough.

"I don't know where to start," she'd said.
"Have you made a list?"
"Yes, but there are too many things on it."
"What are the criteria?"
"Well, it's about the rate of gaseous diffusion in..."
"That's not what I asked. It doesn't matter what it's about. What matters is the critical thinking you apply to the problem. Whenever there's too much information you have to narrow things down. Sort out what's important and what isn't."
"How do I do that?"

"You have to ask yourself the right questions."

What were the right questions? She looked at the list. What would someone gain from starting a war? People who wanted to control things were usually driven by love, power and money. Elizabeth didn't think love factored in here, though some seemed to love war.

Power and money. The list had plenty of people on it who had both. She decided to pick out the top ten. Who had the most wealth, the most toys? In a hierarchy of Alpha males, that person would have serious clout. Who would benefit the most from war? She could find out. Almost everything that mattered was in the computers somewhere.

It was a scary thing to contemplate, the power of electronic surveillance at her fingertips. The government's fingertips. With that kind of power, it should be no problem to learn everything necessary about the members of Cask and Swords. She began searching, using a program Stephanie had written that made Google and the other search engines look like something out of the Stone Age.

It didn't take long for a pattern to emerge. It should have been easy to find what she wanted, but it wasn't turning out that way. She kept running into conflicting data and broken links. She entered a new search focused on a prominent Cask and Swords member.

Several hundred miles north of Virginia, a string of characters appeared on a monitor screen with the location of the Project computer. The server was programmed to respond with code designed to worm its way into the computer of any curious person looking for a particular kind of information.

In Virginia, Stephanie hurried into Harker's office.

"Director, shut your computer down."

Elizabeth turned it off. "What is it, Steph?"

"Someone just tried to break through our firewall while you were on the system," she said. "I blocked it and sent a trace back. What were you looking at?"

"One of the Cask and Swords members. He hosts an annual retreat for them at his summer home in Maine."

"You were using the program I wrote? Not Google?"

"Yes. I wanted a deeper layer."

"Whoever he is, someone with serious computer savvy is working for him. My program triggered an auto response that tried to send a virus back to you. I quarantined it."

"It's not a standard security response?"

"No way. My program is transparent. I designed it to get through the firewalls at the Pentagon. A normal security program wouldn't respond to it."

"Will they know it was us looking?"

"Yes. To send something back they had to isolate our location, which is almost impossible. I'd like to meet whoever wrote the program."

There was grudging admiration in her voice. Stephanie was a legend in the small world of extreme hackers, where she was known only by her screen name, Wonder Woman. She'd worked for NSA before Elizabeth recruited her.

"This man heads up the richest private investment bank in America," Elizabeth said. "Maybe that explains the security."

"Maybe."

On the list of Cask and Swords members, Elizabeth put an asterisk by the name of Phillip Harrison III.

CHAPTER TWENTY-SEVEN

Selena came into Nick's hotel room with her laptop under her arm. They were sleeping in separate rooms and separate beds. It had nothing to do with being in a Muslim country. Until Nick got a handle on his nightmares, it seemed like a smart move. Neither one of them was happy about it.

"What did you find out?" Nick said.

"What do you know about the Templars?"

"Not a lot. I know they conquered Jerusalem and that they were knights that fought in the crusades."

"The Templars protected the routes to the Holy Land. They invented a banking system as a way to keep pilgrims from being robbed along the way. You gave your money to them and they gave you a piece of paper that was like a credit card. You could use that at Templar stations during your pilgrimage to pay for things. If you were robbed, it was worthless to the robbers. The Order charged interest. It made them wealthy, along with donations of land and money from the nobles and the Church."

"Pretty slick. And here I thought credit cards were a modern development."

"The King of France owed the Templars a lot of money he'd borrowed for his wars. He made a deal with the Pope and accused them of heresy so he could get out of paying."

"I hate to say this, but that sounds pretty modern, too. Like the banks making a deal with the government and blaming the little guy for going in debt."

"Anyway. The Order was disbanded. The leaders were tortured and burned at the stake. They had a large treasure but the King never found it. The Ark may have been part of that."

"Who was the king?"

"Phillip. He was called Phillip the Fair."

They both thought of it at the same time.

"The Fair King in the quatrain," Nick said. "Remember?"

"Yes." She pulled up the quatrain on her laptop.

That which was sought was not found
Fire and death no tongue would loosen
In the land of the fair king
The Pale Rider reigns supreme

"It makes sense," Nick said. "Nostradamus is talking about what happened to the leaders and the Templar treasure. Nobody told the king where it was, even when they were tortured."

"The pope and the king died not long after the heresy trials," she said. "Jacques de Molay predicted their deaths as they lit the flames under him."

"The Pale Rider reigns Supreme," Nick said.

"That manuscript is like a sentence of death for anyone who has it. There are a lot of people who want that treasure. Not to mention the Ark."

"We're the ones who have it now."

"You had to say that." She pushed hair away with the back of her hand.

"People will keep after us until we find the Ark or prove it doesn't exist. You said you found something. What is it?"

"The Templars had branches all over Europe, especially in England and France. I came across a medieval reference to a place called the House of Five Trees. It's a chapel in Normandy."

"Another tourist attraction?"

"No. I had some trouble locating it. It's off the beaten track and it was never an important site, not like some of the Templar buildings. It's just a small chapel in ruins, not much to see."

"Another stamp for the passport. I'll call Harker."

On the second ring she picked up.

"Yes, Nick."

"We need to go to France." He told her what Selena had discovered. "The chapel is in the countryside near Cherbourg."

"All right. Do it as soon as you can."

"There's an Air France flight to Paris tomorrow."

"Try to stay out of trouble."

"Roger that." He hung up.

"How about a glass of wine?" Selena said. She held up a bottle. "Chardonnay."

"I'll get some ice. There's a machine in the hall. It'll just take a minute."

Nick picked up the ice bucket and went into the hall. The machine was at the end of the corridor, set back in an alcove. The hall was carpeted in a floral pattern. It was a big hotel. Rows of doors marched down both sides of the corridor.

He got to the machine and slid the lid open and reached for the scoop. As he scraped the ice into the scoop, he heard a soft sound.

Something hit him.

CHAPTER TWENTY-EIGHT

Nick opened his eyes. He was dizzy. The room moved, his vision blurred. He was lying on his side on carpet. His hands were bound with duct tape. Something sticky had trickled down over his ear. Pain pounded behind his eyes. He was in one of the hotel rooms. It was dimly lit. He could see four legs in long pants and two pairs of feet, two sets of brown shoes with thick, quiet rubber soles.

Suckered. His hands felt numb. The tape was cutting off circulation. *Why didn't I sense them?*

"He's awake."

"Get him in the chair."

American accents. How long has it been? The others will be looking for me.

The chances they would find him weren't good.

Someone grabbed him under his armpits and lifted him onto a straight back wooden chair. Duct tape went around his body, pinning him to the chair. His vision cleared. The headache got worse, like nails being pounded into his skull.

The man who had taped him to the chair was short, stocky, with a face that looked like it had been in more than a few bar fights. Nick could smell his breath, loaded with garlic and something unpleasant. He spoke with the sound of the street.

"He don't look so tough," he said.

"You're not getting paid to think about how he looks." The voice was cultured and came from behind him. Nick had heard it somewhere. Then he remembered. Anderson, the attaché at the Embassy.

As if reading his mind, Anderson stepped in front of him, letting himself be seen. It meant they were going to kill him. Nick's adrenaline kicked in.

"You're thinking your friends will find you in time," Anderson said. "That isn't going to happen."

"What do you want?"

"Come on, Carter, you know what I want. Where is the Ark?"

"I don't know where it is. If I did, I wouldn't be here, would I?"

Anderson squatted down in front of him and looked Nick in the eyes. "Let me tell you what's going to happen. You're going to tell me what you know. We can do it the easy way or the hard way."

"You don't have a better line than that?"

"This is Willy," Anderson said. He gestured at the other man. "Willy likes to hurt people. Right, Willy?"

"Yes, Mister Anderson."

"The first thing he'll do is break your fingers."

"Fuck you, Anderson."

"Now who needs a better line?"

They hadn't bound his legs. Nick ducked his head and launched himself at Anderson, still squatting in front of him. The back of the chair caught him over the nose. It was a satisfying sound. Anderson went down like a stone. Nick rolled over him and slammed into Willy's legs. The man fell down, flailing. Nick tried to get up, but Willy was quicker. Nick saw the shoe coming at him but couldn't get out of the way in time. Everything went black.

CHAPTER TWENTY-NINE

Selena knew something was wrong when Nick wasn't back in a few minutes. She called Ronnie and Lamont. Now the three of them stood at the end of the hall by the ice machine.

"They can't have taken him far," Ronnie said. "How long's it been? Ten, fifteen minutes?"

"That's time enough." Lamont paced back and forth. "Look, I was down in the lobby. If they'd gone out the front, I would have seen them."

"Plenty of other ways. Back entrance, the laundry, through the kitchen."

"That would cause a stir," Selena said. "You know he wouldn't go without finding a way to stop them."

"If they had a gun in his ribs..." Ronnie said. "No, he'd find a way around that."

"They had to knock him cold," Lamont said. "If he'd been conscious there'd be signs of a fight."

"Hard to go unnoticed if you're dragging someone through the kitchen," Ronnie said.

"Maybe he's still in the hotel," Selena said.

"If he is, they couldn't take a chance on being seen in the elevator." Lamont stopped pacing. "Either the stairs or he's still on this floor."

"It would have to be a room close to the ice machine," Selena said. "Same reason. They wouldn't risk dragging him down a long hall like this. Someone might see it."

"If they've got him out in the city we won't find him," Ronnie said. "Our only shot is if he's still here."

He looked at the long row of doors. "Selena, take the right. Lamont, you take the left, I'll go down the middle. Look for marks, anything. If they dragged him it might show up on the rug."

They began working their way quietly down the corridor. Ten doors down on the right, Selena held up her hand. She gestured at the floor. There was a soft indentation, barely visible, where something had been dragged across the threshold. She knelt down. There was tiny drop of blood on the carpet. She took out her gun and placed her ear against the door. Ronnie and Lamont came over, pistols in hand. There was a murmur of voices inside.

"*That son of a bitch.*"

"*You all right, Mister Anderson?*"

"No, I'm not all right."

"What do you want to do?"

"We're wasting time. Wake him up. Tape his mouth and then hurt him. He'll talk."

Selena stood and whispered in Ronnie's ear. "In there. At least two."

Ronnie nodded. He stepped back and wound himself around like a discus thrower and slammed his foot into the door. The frame splintered. He kicked again and the door flew open.

Selena took in the scene. Nick was unconscious, slumped over and bound to a chair with silver tape. A stocky man had a gun in his hand. A second, taller man stood near, reaching under his jacket.

Lamont fired first, past Selena's ear, the noise of the shot deafening. She felt the heat as the gun fired. She fired at the tall man, twice. He had a pistol in his hand and was bringing it up as she pulled the trigger. The bullets struck him in the chest and drove him back across the bed.

The stocky one got off a shot. Lamont grunted. Ronnie fired, three quick shots. The man staggered back against the wall and fell to the floor.

The room stank of gunpowder and sweat and blood. The tall man lay on the bed, leaking blood. He wasn't moving. His eyes were open. The man Ronnie had shot was crumpled against the wall, dead. Selena went over to Nick.

Lamont slid down in the doorway. He coughed and blood came out of his mouth. He clasped his hand across a bloody hole in his chest. Air whistled between his fingers, an unpleasant, sucking sound.

Ronnie knelt beside him. "Hold on, Lamont. Hold on."

Shit! Selena thought. She pulled out her phone.

CHAPTER THIRTY

Elizabeth couldn't remember being this angry. Lamont was in critical condition. Nick had a bad concussion. The Jordanians were in an uproar. It didn't help that one of the bad guys was accredited to the US Embassy and worked for Langley. It had the makings of a full blown diplomatic incident.

Earlier, she'd briefed the President. Rice had been calm, but incidents like this jeopardized the existence of the Project. Jordan was technically an ally in the Middle East, and there were few enough of those. He'd agreed to put pressure on the Jordanians to get her team airlifted to Ramstein AFB in Germany, where there was American medical care. She was on thin ice with the White House and she knew it.

All because of an artifact that might not even exist and an arrogant bunch of privileged narcissists who had never made it past their adolescent fantasies of power and imperial glory. *A secret society, for God's sake. Maybe they had a big tree house somewhere, too.* Sometimes she wondered how America had managed to get as far as it had, with people like them running things. It bothered her, a lot. She believed in her country, but these men were a cancer eating away at the foundation of everything she believed in.

Still, she had a job to do. Americans needed protection from the forces that wanted to destroy their way of life. If Cask and Swords was any indication, they needed protection from some of their own leaders.

Stephanie came into Elizabeth's office.

"The President came through," she said. "I just spoke with Selena. The Jordanians have declared everyone Persona Non Grata. They've been escorted to a Jordanian Air base. A C-130 is picking them up as we speak."

"'How is Lamont?"

"Not good. He took one through a lung."

"Steph, whatever else happens, I'm going to take these bastards down."

"I don't think you'll get any argument from the others."

"This banker. Harrison. He seems to be a key figure in Cask and Swords. I want full surveillance on him."

"What about the legalities?"

"Put a smoke screen around it. Use the National Security ploy and that judge in Alexandria. Do it by the book, but get it in place."

"And if we can't do it by the book?"

Elizabeth looked out at the flowers. She knew what her father would say, if he were alive.

You're on a slippery slope, Elizabeth. What about the rules of law? You can't break the rules just because there are others who don't follow them. If you act illegally because you think it's justified, you're no better than the criminals. Law is the foundation of our Republic.

The problem was that the foundation had been undermined by people like Harrison. People who felt safe because they knew those who believed in the rule of law were constrained by it.

"Elizabeth?" Stephanie waited for her answer.

"Do it anyway."

Stephanie started to say something, then thought better of it. "What about the team? Do you still want them going to France?"

Elizabeth picked up her pen and began drumming on the desk.

"What do you think?"

There was a reason Elizabeth had made Stephanie her deputy. She was smart and savvy enough to take over if she had to. Elizabeth respected her opinion.

"They're high profile now," Steph said. "Everyone is watching them. It might be a good idea to let things cool off some."

Elizabeth set the pen down. "These people have been ahead of us all the way. If there's something in France, they've probably found it. If they haven't, it doesn't matter. I'm going to bring the team home."

"Nick won't like it. He's pretty upset about Lamont."

"He'll get his chance. But now isn't the time to get even. Rice is keeping his distance. This has caused a lot of trouble for him. I can't risk another incident overseas. Not yet."

"What about the CIA connection? Are you planning to talk to Hood?"

Clarence Hood was DCI, head of the Central Intelligence Agency. He and Elizabeth had a good working relationship.

"Yes, but I don't think Anderson was acting under Langley's orders. He was Cask and Swords, class of '99. They're the ones behind it. This man, Harrison. I'm sure he's involved."

"How do you know?"

"Call it intuition."

Stephanie nodded. "That'll work."

CHAPTER THIRTY-ONE

The flight from Jordan to Ramstein took four hours. An ambulance waited on the runway to take Lamont to the Landstuhl Regional Medical Center and straight into surgery. He was out of their hands. At the base, they were assigned rooms reserved for officers passing through.

They met in the Officer's Club for dinner.

"Not bad," Ronnie said. "But the NCO club is friendlier."

Nick had a black eye and swollen face from being kicked in the head. He had flashes of dizziness and a low grade headache. The doctors had told him it was a concussion, as if he didn't already know that. It wasn't the first time.

"What's the plan, Kemo Sabe?" Ronnie sipped a coke.

Nick had an Irish whiskey in his hand. He wasn't supposed to drink, but he didn't give a damn what the doctors said. He took a swallow. It hit him with a soft burst of warmth in his stomach.

"Harker wants us home. She thinks things are too hot right now."

"What about France?" Selena said.

"What about it? That chapel isn't going anywhere. Harker figures Ahmed would have told someone about what we found at Petra and the bad guys already know about it. If they don't, it can wait."

"And Lamont?" Ronnie asked.

"We won't leave until we know he's stable. It shouldn't be more than a day or two. Once he's out of danger, they'll fly him to Bethesda. He's tough. He'll be all right."

"I talked with Stephanie," Selena said. "Elizabeth is really angry about this. She thinks she knows who is behind it."

"Whoever he is, he'd better watch out," Ronnie said. "You don't want Harker mad at you."

Nick smiled. "No, you don't."

Later, back in her temporary quarters, Selena was getting ready for bed. Nick's room was in another part of the building.

She wrapped herself in a white robe and stood in front of the bathroom mirror, drying her hair. There were deep shadows under her eyes, lines of fatigue on her face. She ran her fingers through her hair. The Jordanian sun had brought out red highlights, rose red like the rocks in Petra, mixed with the blond.

Her 35th birthday was coming up. Not exactly over the hill, but the stress of the job was beginning to show. There was tension in her face that hadn't been there a year ago. *Still looking good, though*, she thought. *At least that's not a problem. Not yet.*

She let the robe fall open. She ran her fingers over the puckered scar low down on her abdomen where a bullet had nearly killed her. She let the robe slip to the floor and turned, looking over her shoulder. The scar where the bullet had exited was a rough, red ripple on her skin, next to a white line that reached to her buttocks and marked where the surgeons had gone in to repair her spine.

The weight she'd put on after being shot was almost gone, now that she could work out again. Physically she felt a lot like her old self. The mental part was a different story.

Something had changed. The jacketed round that almost paralyzed her had done more than put her in a hospital. It had left her with a sense of vulnerability that hadn't been there before. Before Mexico she'd felt she could handle anything, even after the close calls that had filled her life since she'd joined the Project. She was strong. She was skilled. She could kick ass. And now she knew that she could die just as quickly as the weakest person on the planet. Worse, she could be crippled for life. All it took was a well-placed bullet.

She wasn't like Nick and the others. Maybe it was their military background, some male thing. Whatever it was, the idea they might get killed didn't seem to bother them. They never talked about it. They didn't seem to worry about it.

Since Mexico, she worried about it. She covered her feelings up with flip remarks or black humor. Come to think of it, that was what they did, Nick and Ronnie and Lamont. She remembered Nick had told her black humor helped, back when she'd first joined the team. So maybe they felt the same way she did, they just didn't talk about it. Like her.

The thought was comforting, somehow.

She turned out the light.

She wished Nick was lying next to her.

Sleep wouldn't come.

CHAPTER THIRTY-TWO

"A cat?"

Elizabeth looked at the huge orange cat in Selena's arms. His ear was tattered and torn. He had only one front tooth. He drooled. He sounded like a truck in need of a tune up.

"That's not a cat. It's a fugitive from a zoo. You want it to live here?"

"He's not just any cat," Selena said. "Burps is a hero. He saved our lives in California."

"That cat," Elizabeth said. "The one that makes noises."

"Only when he eats too much. He won't be any trouble. Burps is an outdoor cat. He'll keep the moles out of the flowers. Steph and I will take care of him."

"I couldn't leave him in California," Nick said. "Think of him as added security. A watch cat."

"We need a mascot," Stephanie said. "A good luck mascot."

"I think he should live here," Ronnie said. "It lightens things up a little. I can make a cat door for the tool shed. He could go in there when the weather's bad."

Elizabeth knew when she was outnumbered. "All right."

Burps had been watching her. He purred louder. The sound rumbled across the room.

"See?" Selena said. "He knows. He's a very smart cat."

She carried the cat over to the garden doors and set him down. She opened the door. Burps looked, walked outside and sat down. He began cleaning his paw. Selena closed the door.

"I talked with Lamont's doctors," Elizabeth said. "They're keeping him in Germany for another day, then they're sending him back here to Bethesda. But he's out of commission for a while."

"What happens now?" Nick said.

"If Adam is right, Cask and Swords is behind this. The man at the center of that is a banker named Harrison. I've got full electronic surveillance on him. Most of the time we know what he's doing."

"Most of the time?"

"He uses an encrypted sat phone sometimes. I don't think he's talking about banking. Speaking of which, Stephanie managed to look at the offshore accounts where he keeps most of the money. Tell them what you found out, Steph."

"Harrison's main accounts are in the British Virgin Islands and the Caymans. That gives him a nice, legal tax dodge. The accounts are set up in shell companies with several layers of separation from Harrison. He's heavily invested in defense industries, gas and oil and real estate. His bank did quite well with the financial meltdown and the government money that went out. He's also funding a few foreign politicians."

"Can he do that?"

"As a private individual, yes. The main recipient is an Israeli politician named Weisner. He's the leader of an extremist right wing party that wants to reclaim the West Bank and Gaza and kick all the Arabs out of Israel. He also advocates using nukes against Iran."

"There's an election coming up in Israel," Elizabeth said. "Weisner is a serious contender to become the next Prime Minister."

"Why would Harrison back someone like that?" Nick asked.

"Weisner's policies could start another war. War means big bucks for Harrison and his friends. Harrison has made several public statements attacking Islam. A war over there with a lot of Muslim casualties would appeal to him."

"Where does the Ark come in?" Ronnie said.

"If the Ark turns up, Weisner would use it to beat the drums for war. For what it's worth, his first name is Joshua."

"So the Arab world is the new Jericho?"

"It might as well be, as far as he's concerned."

"Son of a bitch," Nick said. They all looked at him.

"Now I know what Herzog wasn't telling me, back in Jordan."

"What do you mean?" Elizabeth said.

"When we were talking, I got the feeling he wasn't telling us something. He must know Harrison is backing this guy. Why didn't he want us to know?"

"He probably didn't want to air Israel's dirty laundry," Elizabeth said. "Strictly speaking, it wasn't necessary for you to know. It's not directly related to finding the Ark."

Nick felt his blood pressure rising. "It would have saved us some time if he'd pointed us at Harrison."

"Whatever we may think, we don't have proof yet about Harrison's involvement with Bertrand's murder and the attacks on you," Elizabeth said. "Until we have it, there isn't a lot we can do."

"There's something I can do."

"What?"

"Talk to Herzog."

CHAPTER THIRTY-THREE

Ari Herzog's office was on the top floor of Shin Bet HQ in New Jerusalem. His rank rated a large room and a window looking out to the Old City and the Temple Mount, a sight he never grew tired of seeing. Ari was finishing up a report on an operation that had stopped four Hezbollah suicide bombers from carrying out an attack on the Mount. In some nations a success like that would have earned the man in charge a medal. In Israel, it was part of a normal day's work. Medals weren't important to Ari. The security of Israel was. He was good at it. That was reward enough.

His phone rang, the private number few had.

"Ari, it's Nick."

I wondered how long it would take. "Nick, how are you?"

"I've been better."

"I heard about what happened in Jordan. I was sorry to hear about your man. Will he recover?"

"He's doing okay. It'll be a while before he's back in action." There was a pause. "You know why I'm calling," he said. It wasn't a question.

Ari sighed. "You are on a secure line?"

"Yes."

"You are calling about the Ark?"

"Damn it. Ari, why didn't you tell us Americans were involved?"

"I wasn't sure."

"So it wasn't because of Weisner?"

"You've been busy, Nick." No point in denying it. "Yes, it was partly about Weisner, Also, as I said, I wasn't sure."

"We're supposed to be allies. You want Harker to keep you up to speed on the Ark, what we find, but you're not willing to tell me who might be behind it on our end? Come on, Ari, that's not going to fly."

"Your country and mine don't always agree. You know I will put mine first. As you must do with yours. I had specific orders regarding Weisner from the Prime Minister. I couldn't tell you. Now I can."

"So tell me."

"If Weisner is discredited, his party will lose the majority of their seats in the Knesset. It will fragment. That is a desirable outcome, from the PM's point of view. We need proof of Weisner's corruption, his collusion with your American banker. Then we will reveal it to the public. It would swing the election."

"This is all about politics?"

"Not entirely, Nick. The Ark is more important. I was confident you would discover the American connection, sooner or later. It seemed like a better way. Would you have believed me if I had told you I suspected one of the most important men in America was trying to kill you? That he didn't want you to succeed?"

"Probably not. But we would have followed up on it. You didn't trust us to keep the part about Weisner to ourselves."

"I apologize, for what it's worth."

There was a brief pause. "All right. Accepted. We'll move on."

"What have you discovered about the Ark?"

"We still don't know where it is. There's a Templar connection. It could even be part of a bigger hoard, if it exists."

"The Templar treasure?"

"Yes."

"You realize what it would mean to find that?" Ari said.

"Aside from the fact that I wouldn't get to keep it? Yeah, I understand. It'll kick up a shit storm. Especially if the Ark is part of it."

"That may be the understatement of the year," Ari said.

After a few more minutes of conversation, Nick signed off. Ari sat for a few moments, thinking about the Ark. Thinking about the Americans. Then he paged Lev.

CHAPTER THIRTY-FOUR

Selena pulled open one of the big glass street doors and walked into her building. She wore a light silk jacket that concealed her pistol, a lavender silk blouse and black pants that matched her low-heeled shoes. The lobby was all marble and glass. It was an elegant building that spoke of wealth. A security desk with a bank of monitors faced the main doors. The desk was manned 24 hours a day, every day, for the peace of mind of the tenants. The guard called to her as she headed for the elevators.

"Doctor Connor, got something for you." He held up a flat package. "International delivery."

She took the package and recognized the writing of Jean-Paul. It sent a jolt of adrenaline through her. Her heart skipped a beat.

"Thank you."

She got in the elevator and punched in the top floor. The doors closed. She resisted the urge to tear the package open. In her condo she went to the kitchen counter. She took her holster and gun and laid them down on the cool granite. She pulled up a stool and opened the package. Inside was another file folder like the one Bertrand had sent in Paris. She untied the string and pulled it open and recognized the cramped writing of Nostradamus.

It was a different document, the missing quatrains, the ones that should have been with the others. Jean-Paul had split the manuscript into two parts. It had been sent to her by low priority, which explained why it had taken this long to reach her. Bertrand had been killed two weeks before. A lot had happened since then.

There was no note with the package.

She looked at the first quatrain. In her mind, she shifted into the peculiar language of Nostradamus.

> *Under a broken sword a great treasure lies*
> *He who gave hostage to the King speaks from the grave*
> *Eight lie beside him*
> *Three seek his wisdom*

I have no idea what this is about. Why couldn't he just say what he means, for once? She read the next quatrain.

> *The army begins the return from the far lands*
> *War waits in a different place*
> *Under the banners of the Eagle, the Star and the Crescent*
> *False gods and retribution supreme*

That one was clearer. The eagle, the star and the crescent. America was the eagle. The star was probably Israel. She couldn't think of another country so identified with a star, except maybe North Korea. The crescent had to refer to a Muslim nation. Iran? Saudi Arabia? All of them?

Troop withdrawals were underway in Afghanistan. Returning from far lands. She felt a shiver run down her spine. It was as if Nostradamus was standing behind her, looking over her shoulder. If he was right, if she understood the prophecy correctly, then a new war was waiting to happen.

There were more quatrains. It would take time to translate them. Selena decided to take the manuscript to Project headquarters so she could work on it with Stephanie. Elizabeth and the others needed to know about this. But before she did that, she thought she might as well make a copy for studying here.

She took the document over to her computer and scanner and began transferring it to electronic files. Ten minutes later she was finished. She copied it to her email and sent it to Stephanie. She turned off the computer and put the manuscript back in the file folder. She put the folder in a black leather briefcase. She clipped her holster back on, closed the door behind her and walked to the elevator.

Selena watched the numbers change as the elevator rose to her floor, thinking about the quatrains. The doors of the elevator opened. She got in and pressed the button for the ground floor. The elevator descended, smooth, efficient.

The doors opened onto the lobby. It took a second to notice that the guard was not at his station. A tiny alarm went off in her head. *There's always someone at the desk*, she thought. *Always.*

Instinct and training saved her. As she stepped from the elevator someone swung a club at her from the right. She moved and took the blow on her shoulder. Her arm went numb. The briefcase was in her left hand. She swung it around in a fast arc, more to distract than injure. The man grunted and blocked the blow. Selena bent and kicked and landed a solid hit on his chest. He grunted again and swung the club at her. She dodged, let go of the briefcase, spun and threw her left elbow into his face, followed with a knee to the groin, slammed the hardened edge of her left hand against the side of his neck. She felt bone break under the blow.

He went down. Out of the corner of her eye, she saw two more men coming for her. Her right arm was still numb and useless. She couldn't draw her pistol. She ran for the stairwell door on the side of the lobby and pushed it open. The body of the guard lay crumpled at the foot of the stairs. She ran up three steps and turned as one of the men came through the door. She launched herself from the steps and caught him with both feet under his chin. His head snapped backward. She heard the bones crack. She fell hard onto her back on the cement floor. It knocked the breath out of her. Gasping, she climbed to her feet.

The door to the lobby stayed closed. Feeling came back in her arm. Her fingers tingled, but she had control again. She drew her pistol and took a deep breath. She stepped over the body of the guard and pulled open the door.

The lobby was empty. The man who had clubbed her lay partway in the elevator, his head at an odd angle. There was a two foot length of pipe lying on the lobby floor next to him. *Must be what he hit me with*. The elevator doors were cycling, trying to close against his body. The third man was gone.

So was her briefcase with the Nostradamus file.

CHAPTER THIRTY-FIVE

"The men who went after you were both in the system," Elizabeth said. "Convictions for assault and burglary. One of them just got out after doing five years for armed robbery."

Selena, Ronnie, Nick and Stephanie were in Harker's office. The cat lay sleeping in the sun outside the garden doors.

"Only five?" Ronnie said.

"He got paroled. Good behavior."

"A boy scout," Ronnie said.

"I'm following up with his parole officer. Known connections, all that. I don't expect to find much. We're not cops. We can't track down every low life he might have known."

"Be nice if we could turn up the third guy," Nick said.

"Selena, I'm sending you over to the Metro Police HQ to look at mug shots, on the off chance we can ID him. You'll liaise with a Detective Mark Hanson over there."

"All right."

"How's your arm?"

She flexed her shoulder. "I'm okay. The shoulder's sore."

"You're lucky he didn't break something," Nick said.

"He wasn't fast enough."

Nick smiled.

"This is starting to feel personal," Elizabeth said. "We need to get this resolved."

"Maybe the new Nostradamus material will help," Selena said.

Elizabeth nodded. "It's a good thing you copied it. They want it that badly, there has to be something in it."

"I printed it out," Stephanie said. She handed copies around.

"There are five quatrains that might have something to do with the Ark," Selena said. "I haven't finished all of the rest them yet but these five are grouped together. They could be relevant."

"How many more are there?"

"Another seventeen."

They looked at the quatrains.

Under a broken sword a great treasure lies
He who gave hostage to the King speaks from the grave
Eight lie beside him
Three seek his wisdom

"Under a broken sword," Ronnie read aloud. "What the hell does that mean?"

"I don't know," Selena said. "Someone's dead, that much is clear. And there are eight others with him."

"So it's about nine dead guys."

"Not just any nine dead guys," she said. "Probably nine dead knights."

"How do you get that?"

"The sword. They used to decorate the tombs of medieval knights with a figure of the knight in his armor, with his sword on top."

"Are you thinking what I'm thinking?" Nick said.

Selena nodded. "One of the Knights Templar. After finding those Templar symbols in Jordan, that's the only thing that makes sense."

"That narrows it down some," Elizabeth said. "How many Templar tombs are there?"

"A lot. Even if we find the right one, we still have to make sense of the quatrain. It's like chasing the white rabbit in Alice in Wonderland."

"How does a man speak from his grave?" Nick asked.

"Through writing, or something left behind. I think there might be something inside the tomb itself. Under the sword."

"That's great," Nick said. "First we have to find the right tomb, then we have to open it up on a million to one chance there's something there except bones."

"Do you have a better idea?"

Harker leaned back in her chair. "What about the other quatrains?"

"Nostradamus is predicting a war."

The army begins the return from the far lands
War waits for them in a different place
Under the banners of the Eagle, Star and Crescent
False gods and retribution supreme

"Eagle, star and crescent. America, Israel and the Muslim world."

"War in the Middle East?" Ronnie said.

"Not again," Nick groaned.

"Our troops are coming back from Afghanistan. It's today he's talking about, right now."

"It might refer to what happened when Nick was in Jerusalem," Harker said.

"It could," Selena said. "But this next one bothers me."

In the seventh month no time remains
The prince's calculations anger heaven
Fire over the Holy City, the sun touches the earth
If the Container is found, then success

"The seventh month is July," Selena said. "That's in just a few days. If any of this means anything, if Nostradamus really saw the future, we're running out of time."

Nick's ear began itching. "It's like the one you think is about Hiroshima."

"Yes. That bit about the sun touching the earth. It's how Nostradamus would have thought about a nuclear explosion, if he'd seen it in a vision. The Holy City would be Jerusalem or

Rome. Or even Mecca. He capitalizes the word container. That could be the Ark. It's called the Sacred Container in the Bible. The next quatrain mentions it again."

"Who's the prince?" Ronnie asked.

"The bad guy," Nick said. "He thinks he's got it covered but he's making a mistake."

"Phillip Harrison," Elizabeth said. Her voice was strange.

They looked at her. "What's the matter, Director?" Stephanie said. "You look like you've seen a ghost."

"I just had this very odd feeling," she said. "My intuition says this prince is Harrison. He's planning something bad."

"A nuclear war would qualify," Nick said.

"What about this other one?" Ronnie said, "the one about wine?"

Four will share wine but three will drink
One less to mark the path
The Sacred Container is beyond
That which is desired

"I don't know. But it has to be about the Ark. That would be the only sacred container anyone would think of."

Harker picked up her Mont Blanc and began tapping. "This is the most bizarre investigation I've ever heard of," she said.

It broke the tension. Everyone laughed.

"Nothing new for us," Nick said. "Pyramids, ancient artifacts, we do it all. Why not prophecies?"

"All right," Harker said. "What's the next step?"

"Let me see if I can pin down a Templar tomb that matches the quatrain," Stephanie said.

"Ronnie and I are going over to Bethesda to see Lamont," Nick said.

"And I'll meet with the detective," Selena said. "What was his name?"

"Hanson. Mark Hanson." Elizabeth wrote his phone number on a piece of paper and handed it to her.

"Give him a call. He's expecting you."

CHAPTER THIRTY-SIX

It was a gorgeous summer day on the Maine coast. This time of year, the sun turned unsuspecting visitors red as a Maine lobster in no time flat. The tourist season was in full swing, but on Indian Island there was none of the chaos that marked the vacation spots along the shore.

Phillip Harrison III sat on the shaded porch above the lawn with a glass of good whiskey and thought about what he was planning. So far, things were progressing more or less on schedule. Wiesner's rhetoric of hatred was doing it's work. Through Croft, a difficult transaction with the Iranians had been brought to a successful conclusion. Harrison had arranged the seed of their destruction. It was a delicious irony that the Iranians saw it as the seed of their victory.

It was all about perception. Victory and destruction were two sides of the same coin.

The book that guided Harrison's life was the Bible. Perception had never been a problem for the people of the Bible. Forgiveness of those who resisted the Lord's Will was not encouraged. One of his favorite quotations was from Deuteronomy:

...the Lord thy God shall deliver them before thee; thou shalt smite them, and utterly destroy them; thou shalt make no covenant with them, nor show mercy unto them...

For Phillip Harrison, those words could have been written to describe Islam and all it's adherents.

Harrison considered himself a patriot. The American people had become soft, weak. War was the solution. War hardened a people, gave it purpose, forged the strength of a nation. It was the fire of war that had given birth to the

Republic. It was war that had united it. It was war that had made America supreme in the world.

That supremacy was at risk because of misguided efforts at negotiating peaceful solutions in a world where peace was impossible, with nations that could not be trusted. The current President was a good example of what could happen. He'd failed to exploit his opportunities. He'd had an opportunity to crush the Muslim world and gain the oil fields of the Middle East, but he'd backed away. He was a coward.

Harrison intended to see that mistake put right. The fact that another war would increase his wealth was secondary. Boyd and Croft were focused on wealth, but Harrison was focused on doing God's work. Harrison believed that the Holy Land needed to be cleansed of the stain of Islam and the holy sites of Christianity reclaimed, once and for all. His Puritan ancestors would approve, he was certain.

Harrison watched a motor launch nearing the island, bringing Boyd and Croft from the mainland. He set his glass on the table beside him and walked down to the landing to greet them.

"Phillip, how are you?"

"Well, Arthur, thank you." The three men shook hands. "There's a light lunch waiting in the house."

They walked up the perfect lawn and into the house. Harrison led the way to the conservatory where the food was laid out on white linen. When the servants had left, Harrison began.

"We have the other part of the Nostradamus file."

"Excellent," Croft said. "Were there any problems?"

Harrison sipped his whiskey. "Two units were killed. It's of no importance. They were disposable. The third man showed initiative. I'm moving him up a bit."

"How soon will we have a location?" Boyd asked.

"So far, the clues have been accurate. Once the quatrains are translated, we'll follow up on the new ones. This is the end of the Nostradamus work. If the pattern holds, he put something in there that will give us the right place to look."

"And if the Ark is not there?"

"I am convinced that the Templar treasure at least is within reach," Harrison said. "That alone recommends our present course of action. If the quatrains reveal the Ark as well, so much the better. If not, we'll proceed with our alternative plan."

"The assassinations," Croft said.

"Yes. It shouldn't take more than a few weeks to get the pot boiling. Then we tip it over."

"Why don't we just get on with it?" Boyd said.

Harrison was annoyed. "We've been over this, Stephen. It's much better if we can use the Ark. The fanatics will do our work for us. There won't be any possibility of a trail back here. If there's any chance the Templar hoard still exists, or the Ark, we need to secure that first. Once the war begins it will be much more difficult."

Boyd said, "I suppose you're right, Phillip."

"Of course I am."

"What about the President's group, the Project?"

"They've been annoying, I admit. They're following the same trail we are. They may have a copy of the second part of the manuscript. If they don't, what they do doesn't matter. If they do, we'll be prepared. Next time they don't walk away."

CHAPTER THIRTY-SEVEN

The First District station of the Washington Metro Police was in a converted school building on M Street SW. It housed a state of the art forensic lab, offered community outreach programs and provided evidence storage. The D.C. police needed a lot of storage.

Selena parked her Mercedes next to a row of cruisers with the stylized flag logo of D.C. She put a card on the dash that identified her car as being on government business. Maybe it wouldn't draw a ticket.

The desk sergeant told her to wait for Detective Hanson to come and escort her. The station had a faint, stale odor of fear and stress and sweat, along with the kind of smell that seemed to be poured into institutional buildings with the concrete. After a few minutes a man came through a set of swinging doors on her left. He wore an off the rack gray suit and black shoes and had a pair of thick binders under his arm. He walked over to her. She stood.

"Doctor Connor? I'm Detective Hanson. Thanks for coming down."

He held out his hand. His grip was warm, firm.

Hanson was about Nick's height, six feet tall. He had black hair and blue eyes and a face that looked as though you might not want to get on the wrong side of him. His eyes had the same kind of look as Nick's, as if they'd seen much more than they'd wanted, none of it good. There was a thin scar on the bottom of his chin. She caught a faint whiff of aftershave.

"This way," Hanson said.

He led her through the doors and down a hallway to a room with a table and a large one way window on the wall. There were two chairs. There was a camera on the ceiling. The table was bolted to the floor. Hanson set the binders down on the table.

"Grab a seat. This is one of the rooms we use for interrogations. It's a lot quieter than the squad room and we won't be distracted here. Have you ever done this before?"

His voice was deep, pleasant. Selena liked it.

"No."

"It's straightforward." Hanson opened one of the binders. "These are photos of people you don't want to meet. We've got thousands of them, but I figured the best shot was to pull known associates of the men who attacked you."

He stopped and gave her an appraising look. "That was good work, by the way. Most women would be dead. Hell, most of the men I know would be dead. How did you do it?"

The question made her uncomfortable. "Oh, training. And luck."

"Sorry. I shouldn't have asked."

Sensitive. Who would have guessed? He picked right up on how I felt. An interesting man.

"That's all right. I study martial arts."

"Guess that explains it. Okay." All business, now. "You can see, each page has pictures. Take your time, see if any of them look like the third man who was there. Would you like something to drink? Coffee, a soda?"

"Coffee would be fine."

"How do you take it?"

She felt something stirring. *He's asking you about coffee.* With something of a shock, she realized she was attracted to him. She hadn't been attracted to anyone since she'd met Nick.

"Cream, no sugar."

"Coffee's not great here, but it's hot. I'll be right back."

He left the room. Her thoughts were confused. Something had just happened, and she knew enough about herself to realize she would have to deal with it. But not now. She pulled the book of pictures closer and began studying the photos.

CHAPTER THIRTY-EIGHT

"Him," Selena said.

She put her finger on a photo. She'd been looking at pictures for the past two hours. Hanson had brought more binders in after she'd failed to recognize anyone in the first two.

"You're sure?"

"Yes. I got a good look at him. There's something about his face. Cruel."

The man in the photo had wide ears that stuck out from his head and eyes that looked dead.

"Elbert Sturrock. Armed robbery, assault, attempted murder. He did fifteen upstate. Got out about six months ago."

"Why do they keep letting these people out?" she said.

"You shouldn't ask a cop that, unless you want to see him get mad." Hanson smiled. "Politics, budgets and do-gooders, mostly. Loopholes in the law and bottom feeding lawyers that exploit them."

He closed the binder. "Now that we have an ID, we'll find him. We get him in here, we can sweat him a little."

"You think you can find out who hired him?"

"I'll do my best." Hanson looked at his watch. "I'm off in ten. How about a drink? There's a place a couple of blocks away."

Why not? she thought. Then, *No.*

"Not today. Maybe another time." *Why had she said that? She'd left the door open, just a crack.*

Hanson kept the disappointment out of his voice. "Another time would be great. You have a number I can reach you at? I'll let you know what we find out."

"You have a piece of paper?"

Are you really going to give him your number?

Hanson took out a notebook, handed it to her. She wrote down a number. It wasn't the number Nick and the others used to reach her. "It goes to a machine," she said. "I don't usually pick up. Just leave a message."

Back out on the street, she wondered what she was doing.

CHAPTER THIRTY-NINE

Elizabeth came into her office. Burps was asleep on her chair, drooling. She'd never been a cat person. Even so, she found the presence of the cat comforting. There was something about this ragged lump of orange that she liked. She lifted him off the chair and walked over to the garden door and set him down. She opened the door.

"Go," she said. She pointed.

Burps looked at her, yawned and moved leisurely into the garden. She closed the door. She used a tissue to wipe off her chair and sat down. The others came into the room and took seats.

"I think I know who Nostradamus meant," Stephanie said, "in the lines about giving a hostage and all that." She looked pleased with herself.

"Who is it?" Selena asked.

"If I'm right, the first Earl of Pembroke, William Marshal. He's buried in the nave of Temple Church, in London." She pulled up a picture on the big monitor. It showed a damaged stone figure of a knight in mail lying on his back. His right hand grasped his sword. The stone blade was broken.

"He was a Templar?"

"Yes."

"Why do you think it's him?" Harker asked.

"Marshal was one of the most powerful men in England. His son was held hostage by King John to make sure he stayed loyal. That fits with the quatrain. And he's holding a broken sword. If that isn't enough, his effigy is one of nine. There are eight others in the Temple Church, all close by, all Templar knights."

"Temple Church is famous, a big tourist attraction," Selena said. "It was the London Templar headquarters when they were at the height of their power."

"When did this guy die?" Ronnie asked.

"1219," Stephanie answered. "He was the real thing. His life could be the model for the heroic knight."

"Doesn't do him much good now," Ronnie said. "All he's got is a fancy tomb to show for it."

"One day they could make one for you, Ronnie," Nick said. "Carve out a grenade launcher instead of a sword."

"That's enough," Elizabeth said. "How are we going to find out what's in that tomb?"

"Pretty clear. Nostradamus says there's something there. We have to get into the church and open it."

Elizabeth coughed into a tissue. "Let me get this straight," she said. "You want to break into a major English historical attraction, vandalize a famous tomb with a slab on it that probably weighs hundreds of pounds and root through the bones or whatever, all in hope of finding a clue that might not even be there."

Nick nodded. "That's about right."

Elizabeth sighed. "There will be guards. You can't hurt them."

"We'll think of something," Nick said.

CHAPTER FORTY

"How do we know which one is Pembroke?" Nick asked.

"The tombs are marked," Selena said. "We just read the signs."

They stood in the circular nave of Temple Church in London. It was three in the afternoon. Sunlight streamed through tall, stained glass windows, throwing spatters of rainbow light on the stone floor and across the silent effigies of the Templar knights.

Temple Church had two sections, the round nave and a larger, rectangular chancel, built a half century later. From the air, the building looked like a giant exclamation point laid down between Fleet Street and the Thames River, with the round Templar church forming the dot.

The building was a fine example of gothic architecture. The ceiling of the church was arched and groined. Arched alcoves completely circled the nave. The wall above the alcoves was decorated by a continuous row of stone faces that leered out with grotesque expressions. The eyes seemed to follow Nick around the room.

The nine effigies of Templar knights lay on the floor in the middle of the nave. A central, round tower rose above, supported by arches of stone and massive columns of dark marble. High overhead, the ceiling of the tower was made of closely fitted wood.

Each tomb was identified with a simple black sign etched in white. They found the one for William Marshal. The effigy was damaged with the passage of 900 years, the stone sword broken in several places. His face looked tired, worn. A line of white ran all around the carved slab.

"It's cemented down," Ronnie said. He kept his voice low. "No way it moves without making a lot of noise."

"We figured on that," Nick said. "The seal is probably not very thick, just enough to keep it in place."

"We might get in through that door." Ronnie nodded at a wooden door set in the west wall under a circular stained glass window. "It leads outside. We wouldn't have to come through the rest of the building."

"Looks solid. Built to withstand trouble."

"It's a door. We can get through it."

"Is it alarmed?"

They wandered over to the door. Nick couldn't see anything that would trigger an alarm.

"The lock doesn't look modern."

"The door is a replica," Selena said. "The church was bombed during the war. Everything that was made of wood burned. When it was restored they tried to make everything look like the original."

"The lock's not a problem," Ronnie said.

"I've seen enough. Let's go back to the hotel."

On the way out, Nick picked up a plan of the church and a few postcards with pictures of the nave.

CHAPTER FORTY-ONE

Twelve hours later they were back, outside the door opening into the nave. The night was dark except for a distant streetlamp and a faint glow from within the church. Mist from the Thames and an elaborate stone portico outside the entrance helped conceal them. There was no one about. A light rain drifted down.

"Got it," Ronnie said.

Nick heard the tumblers turn. There was no sound of an alarm. No one expected thieves to go after stone slabs that would take six men to carry away.

They wore dark clothes. The tools were in a pack. They carried tranquilizer guns and their pistols. If they ran into someone, the trank guns could take anyone down before they sounded an alarm. They were effective, silent and non-lethal.

Ronnie eased the door open and they slipped inside.

So far, so good, Selena thought. Her heart was beating hard.

The interior of the nave was dimly lit. Deep pools of shadow filled most of the room.

"This feels wrong," Selena said. "Opening this tomb."

"I know. But we have to do it. It's not like we're grave robbers. Watch the entrance from the chancel," Nick said to Selena. His voice was very quiet. "You see a guard coming this way, put him down."

She nodded and moved to the chancel entrance, a trank gun in her hand. Few lights showed in the cavernous building. Rows of pews lined the floor. Several candles burned in the darkness. There was no one in sight.

Nick and Ronnie knelt by the effigy of William Marshal, First Earl of Pembroke. Ronnie took a package out of his pack. He uncoiled a length of sticky black cord and began to lay it all the way around the edge of the slab where it met the floor.

The cord was treated with a compound designed for Special Forces. It reacted with concrete to break down the molecular structure. In effect, it turned concrete to dust. It had to be ignited and made a lot of smoke. It wasn't loud like a demolition charge, but in the deep silence of the nave it was going to be noisy.

"All set." Ronnie stood.

They stepped away from the slab. Ronnie touched off the cord. It burned with a bright, blue-white light and hissed and sparked as it shot around the slab. The noise was like a nest of snakes suddenly wakened. Thick, white smoke drifted up past the soaring arches.

They knelt down by the carved slab and pushed against it. It moved, just a little.

"On three," Nick said. "One, two, three." They grunted and pushed. The heavy slab scraped across the floor, a harsh sound of stone against stone that echoed through the chamber. The tomb of the Earl lay open. They peered in.

"Not looking so hot," Ronnie said.

"What did you expect? He's been dead a long time."

The Earl had been buried in his skirted, chainmail armor. The flesh had long vanished, leaving only bones. The skull gaped at them from within the headpiece. His skeletal fingers clenched a long broad sword, dull and rusted. There was a dry odor of dissolution, a whiff of rust and decay. Most of his tunic was still intact over the mail, the faded red of the Templar cross still visible.

"Look under the sword," Nick said.

Ronnie freed the ancient blade from Pembroke's fingers.

"Nothing. I don't see anything."

"There has to be something. Under his sword, it said. A great treasure."

"Not even a coin."

"Send Selena over. Maybe she can figure it out. You keep watch."

Ronnie got up, went to Selena and whispered. She came over and knelt down over the open crypt.

"He doesn't look so good."

"That's what Ronnie said. We can't find anything."

"You looked under the sword?"

"Yes."

"Is there an inscription on it?"

Nick turned the blade over. "No. Just rust."

"Let me think," she said. "This has to be the right tomb."

Nick waited.

"Nostradamus always played on words...pull up the skirt."

"What?"

"The skirt of his chainmail. Maybe Nostradamus wasn't talking about his broadsword."

Nick smothered a laugh. "How do you come up with these things?"

"I used to read a lot of Shakespeare," she said.

He worked the skirt of mail up around the bones. The mail was heavy and awkward. The right leg came apart under his hands as he moved the armor up over the hips. Fragments of a loin cloth covered something resting in the bony cradle of the pelvis. He pulled out a flat brown leather pouch, dried and cracked. Barely visible was a nobleman's crest, cut into the leather.

"I'll be damned," he said.

At the doorway to the chancel, Ronnie saw something move in the shadows.

"Nick," he hissed. "Someone coming."

Nick placed the pouch in a pocket on his pants. He stood. Selena stood with him.

There was a flash and sharp report in the darkness of the chancel. A bullet ricocheted off the wall near Ronnie's head. He ducked back into the round church.

"More than one," he called. There was no need to be silent now.

A burst of automatic fire from the chancel sent chips of marble flying. Ronnie fired twice into the darkness, loud reports that rang off the stone walls. Nick and Selena ran to the doorway, across from Ronnie. Nick reached around the corner and fired three quick rounds, blind. He risked a glance and saw a man dive behind one of the pews. Shots came from the right side of the church and shattered a stone vase inside the nave.

"Stalemate," he said. "They can't get in here, we can't go out there. They can see us if we try and they've got stuff to hide behind."

Ronnie said, "Too much noise. Someone's bound to hear." He fired three more rounds. More shots came back.

"I count four weapons," Selena said. "Maybe more."

"We've got what we came for. Ronnie, cover us, we're coming across."

Ronnie reached around the opening and fired four shots as Selena and Nick ran across. Bullets hummed past them. A window shattered and littered the floor of the nave with bits of glass.

"We'll go out the door. Like we came in."

"They could be out there," Selena said.

"Be ready in case they are. Lay down fire through the arch into the chancel as we go. Stay as close to the wall as you can. Once we get there, you and I cover while Ronnie opens the door."

"Got it." She nodded.

"Go."

They ran for the exit, firing blindly behind them at the opening into the chancel as they went. The three pistols made a lot of noise. Empty brass bounced and pinged off the floor as they ran. Shots came from behind them. A big chunk blew out of the circular window over the door.

Ronnie pulled the door open. A man appeared behind them at the entrance to the nave. Nick fired twice. The slide locked back on his pistol. The figure fell back into the chancel. They went through the door. Nick pulled it shut behind him, dropped the empty magazine and clicked in another. In the distance, a police siren sounded. Then a second joined in.

There was no one waiting for them outside. They ran in the shadows until they reached the spot where they'd left their rental car and piled in. Nick pulled away. Before he turned the corner, he saw the reflection of the lights on a police car bouncing off the Temple walls. Then the lights were behind them.

He got a few more blocks and slowed down.

"Anyone hit?"

"Negative."

"No," Selena said. The adrenaline rush was still going strong. "How did they know we were there?"

"They might not have known," Nick said. "It has to be the same people who came after you in Washington. They got the manuscript. They figured it out, like we did. Bad luck they showed up when we were there."

"But good luck they didn't get there ahead of us," she said. "I wonder what's in that pouch?"

"We'll find out. Be nice if it isn't another damn puzzle."

CHAPTER FORTY-TWO

Ari Herzog sipped strong black coffee and contemplated the glow of the sun as it reflected from the golden Dome of the Rock. So much beauty. So much hatred. So much history of blood.

Lev came into Herzog's office. He was carrying a newspaper. "You see the London papers today?"

"Not yet."

"Take a look." He handed the paper over. Ari sat down at his desk and looked at the front page.

The lead shouted.

Temple Church Shootout Tomb Vandalized, Guards Murdered

"Temple Church. It has to be about the Ark," Lev said. "Your friends from the Project must have been there."

"And someone else," Herzog said. "Nick and the others would not kill the guards. They don't operate like that. If they're involved, they were in there looking for something and were discovered by the wrong people."

"What would they be looking for?"

"I don't know. Let's ask them."

Herzog picked up his phone and entered Nick's number. He turned on the speaker so Lev could listen. Ari and Nick had worked well together during the disastrous visit of the American President to the Temple Mount. Nick had helped save Israel from destruction, a debt that could never be repaid. There was a bond of trust and respect between the two men that crossed national boundaries.

"Yes."

"Nick, it's Ari. I've got you on speaker and Lev is here with me."

"Ari."

"Were you at the Temple Church recently?"

"I take it you've seen the papers."

"Yes."

"We were there. Not us who snuffed the guards, though."

"I never thought otherwise. I thought you were going to keep me informed, Nick."

"Subject to Director Harker's approval, yes."

"Can you tell me what you were doing in that church?"

"Following up on a lead. I can't tell you much more before I talk with Harker."

"You're not giving me much."

"Ari, you know how it works. I'll tell you what I can, when I can."

"The election here is not far away," Ari said. "Weisner is gaining in the polls. There have been terrorist incidents and it's helping him. Your government does not need Weisner as Prime Minister. Let us help you with this, Nick."

"What do you have in mind? Tell me and I'll run it by Harker."

"Put Lev on your team while you look for the Ark. He can report back to me."

It was the first Lev had heard about it. He had been listening to the conversation sitting slumped in one of Ari's arm chairs. Now he sat up straight, surprised.

"You know we have specialized training, Ari."

"Lev can handle it. He was with the *Sayeret Matkal* before I got him. He has the skills you need."

The Sayeret Matkal were the cream of Israeli Special Forces, as good as anything the Americans or Russians or British had. There wasn't any question Lev would have the skills needed.

Nick considered what Ari had asked him. With Lamont out of action they were one short on the team. With someone coming after them at every opportunity, adding an experienced gun to the team could improve the odds.

"I'll think about it. The political angle complicates things."

"That's all I ask, Nick."

They ended the call.

"You could have asked," Lev said, "before you volunteered me to work with Americans."

"They're not just any Americans," Herzog said. "If Nick takes you on, you're in for an interesting experience."

CHAPTER FORTY-THREE

Nick put out Ari's proposal to the team. Everyone was in Harker's office.

"Lamont's gone for three months or longer," Elizabeth said. "It depends on how fast he heals."

"That's the only reason I'm even considering Ari's proposal," Nick said, "because we're a man short. All of Sayeret Matkal's ops are classified and so is their personnel list, but Steph got into their computers. The man Ari wants us to use has hard core combat and black ops experience. We won't have to break him in. He's got as much training as we do."

"We've done it before," Selena said, "with Arkady."

Arkady Korov was Russian Spetsnaz. He'd been on two missions with the Project, in a bizarre alliance against common enemies.

Harker picked up her Mont Blanc and began tapping. "This is sensitive, politically speaking. Herzog wants us to help him discredit an opponent of the current Prime Minister. He's drawing us into the domestic politics of a foreign nation."

"It wouldn't be the first time we did that," Nick said, "but for Ari it's secondary. Finding the Ark and bringing it back to Israel is more important to him. It's true there's a political stink on this. If Weisner gets the Ark he'll use it to bolster his authority to do what he wants. What he wants isn't in our best interest. The fact that Harrison is backing him proves that, if nothing else."

Elizabeth set her pen down. She rubbed her forehead. "Are those headaches of yours catching?" she said. "Because this is giving me one."

They laughed. "Want some aspirin?" Nick said.

"It will take more than that. Ronnie, what do you think? About bringing in Herzog's man?"

"It worked out with Korov," Ronnie said. "Hell, I might have been killed if he hadn't been there. Without Lamont we're stretched kind of thin. I'm for it."

"Selena?"

"It will make us stronger. Yes, I'm for it."

"Nick?"

"What about Herzog? Everything we do will get reported back to him."

"I don't think it matters anymore. It could be to our advantage. This way, we won't have to worry that the Israelis might do something rash while they're trying to find out what we're doing."

"All right," Nick said. "I'll call Ari."

"That's settled, then. Let's talk about what you found in the church."

"What was in the pouch was a letter from Jacques de Molay," Selena said.

Elizabeth had thought nothing else about this search for the Ark could surprise her until she heard that. She considered what Selena had just said.

"The Grand Master of the Templars?"

"The same. It's an extraordinary letter. It was written in Latin. The pouch was sealed with something that kept it tight, so the parchment was in good condition. It's downstairs, in the safe. I've got the translation here."

She read from a piece of yellow note paper.

In the Year of Our Lord, 1307, in the Sixth Month
To Walter de la More, Master and Commander
I, Jacques de Molay, swear by Almighty God that the accusations against the Order are false and without merit. Brother, the King has corrupted the Vicar of Christ. Phillip is not worthy of his throne, nor Clement to hold the Shepherd's Crook. These words alone condemn me to the stake if they are discovered.

You received the shipments from Cyprus, this has been reported to me. I trust you have secured them.

There are rumors Clement will convene an inquiry. I am uncertain what will happen, but fear the King is set to move against us.

Our enemies are many and strong. You must prepare for an assault. The protection of the Container is a charge given to us by Him who rules all. We must keep it from the hands of those who serve the Great Deceiver. The burden is no longer mine, but yours.

May God keep you safe.

"It's signed by de Molay."

"Wasn't he burned at the stake in 1307?" Nick asked.

"No. He was imprisoned, but he wasn't burned until 1314. 1307 is when he and the Templars were arrested. The letter was written in June of 1307. Pope Clement V held an inquiry in August and the Templars were arrested in October."

"The Vicar of Christ in the letter."

Selena nodded.

"Who was Walter de la More?"

"Master of the London Commandery, the Temple Church. He's probably the one who put that pouch in Marshal's tomb. La More was arrested in 1308 and imprisoned in the Tower of London. He wouldn't sign a confession, so he was tortured. He died in the Tower."

"How does Cyprus come into this?" Ronnie asked.

"The main headquarters of the Templars were on Cyprus," Selena said. "The treasury of the Templars was there as well."

"So de Molay knew things were going south and he shipped the Ark to England," Nick said.

"It looks like it. It would have been vulnerable in Cyprus because of Turkish attacks. Likewise in France because of King Phillip. England would have looked like a better bet. They didn't find a great treasure in Cyprus, just a relatively small amount. Perhaps de Molay shipped that to England as well."

"This is all real interesting," Ronnie said, "but we still don't know where it is. We're out of leads."

"But now we have proof the Ark still existed before 1307 and that the Templars had it," Elizabeth said. "It's probably still wherever la More hid it, or it would have surfaced by now."

"Somewhere in England?" Nick said.

"That seems logical." Elizabeth said. "I suppose it could also be in Ireland or Scotland."

"How are we going to pin it down?" Stephanie asked.

"I want you and Selena to research everything you can think of about la More. There has to be something, somewhere. People are predictable. He would have hidden it in a place he thought no one could find, but he would have had some knowledge of wherever that was. So look for patterns. Look at his genealogy, his family, all of it."

"He may have been childless," Selena said. "The Templars took a vow of chastity."

"That doesn't mean he didn't have children," Harker said. "Look anyway."

CHAPTER FORTY-FOUR

Selena saw the red light flashing on her answering machine as she came in the door. Usually the only calls on that line were telemarketers ignoring the do not call rule. She thought there was probably a special place in a particularly hot corner of hell for them and all their employers.

One message. She pressed the play button, ready to delete.

"Hi, Doctor Connor, this is Detective Hanson. Uh, sorry I didn't catch you in." There was a pause. *"Anyway, I wanted to let you know there's nothing new yet on the guy who attacked you. I'd still like to have that drink with you. Give me a call, if you're up for it."*

Hanson read off his phone number. The message ended.

Selena erased it, got a glass out of the cabinet and poured herself an Irish whiskey, a taste she'd picked up from hanging out with Nick. The liquor was strong and warm going down. She walked over to the couch and sat down.

She wasn't going to have a drink with Detective Hanson. What bothered her was that part of her wanted to. She didn't need that kind of complication right now. She took another swallow of whiskey.

Nick.

What did she want from him, exactly?

They weren't sleeping in the same bed anymore and it wasn't helping things between them. His nightmares made it impossible. He hadn't said much about his counseling sessions. She wasn't sure when he was going again. Something always seemed to come up.

She felt like she was treading water, waiting for something to happen that would define them as a couple, one way or another. Everything felt impermanent. She supposed there were worse things. They made a good team in the field and neither one of them would still be alive except for the other. It made for a strong bond. Just the same, knowing he could be killed made it hard to imagine a future together.

Working for the Project wasn't like it had been in the beginning, before she understood what it was really about. It was hard, dirty work, where people got killed. Where her friends were at risk. Where vicious and pathological enemies would do anything to get what they wanted.

She loved Nick, she was certain. She was pretty sure he loved her, but they were different in so many ways. Shared danger gave them something in common. But a relationship needed something more than shared danger to survive.

What about children? She had avoided thinking about children. The kind of work she did, Nick did, it wasn't a good situation for having kids. But she was almost 35. The old cliché about the biological clock popped into her mind. How much longer could she wait? Did she want children or not? If she didn't have children, her family line would stop. Cease to exist. Just like the Earl of Pembroke.

When the detective had asked for her number, she'd had a sudden image of the two of them in bed together. In some ways Hanson was like Nick. Strong, dark-haired, competent, unafraid. A rugged man who carried a gun.

Are you that shallow? she thought. *Dark hair and a gun is enough to turn you on?* She thought about Nick. A wave of unease swept through her. *He could be killed, any time, any day. I could lose him in an instant. I've been pushing it away. How can I give everything over to someone who might leave me forever at any moment?*

The next thought chilled her. *He has to feel the same way about me. He already lost one lover.*

For the first time, she sensed the fundamental problem between them. In her heart, she believed that whatever they had couldn't last. Not because he would leave her for another, or because she wanted someone else. Because a bullet or a bomb could snuff out either one of their lives in an instant.

It felt like someone had thrown a bucket of ice water over her.

There was nothing to do but take it one day at a time. The thought didn't make her feel better, but she could handle one day at a time. At least she could handle it today.

She got up and poured another drink.

CHAPTER FORTY-FIVE

Lev Gefen sat in Harker's office and wondered how this was going to work out. All he knew about the Project was what Ari had told him and what he'd learned from the intelligence files. Like all Special Forces personnel everywhere, he was sure no one else was as good as his own unit, though he had to admit the Project knew what they were doing. Either that, or they were damn lucky. Good units made their own luck.

"I've reviewed your record," Elizabeth said. "I think you'll fit in."

"Those files are classified."

"Yes, they are." She offered no explanation. "Do you have questions for us?"

"Who will be in command in the field?"

"Nick is in command," Elizabeth said. "If he's unavailable, then Ronnie or Selena will take over."

Gefen looked uncomfortable. "I mean no disrespect, but she does not have the same experience as the rest of us. In combat she would be at a disadvantage. Especially hand to hand."

Elizabeth's voice took on an edge. "Selena has proved herself as capable as anyone else on the team."

Selena bit back her first thoughts. "Perhaps you'd like to practice a little hand to hand in the gym?" she said. "Just a friendly match. No pads."

"I am considered expert in Krav Maga," Gefen said. "It wouldn't be fair."

Krav was a highly effective martial art developed by Lev's own Israeli Commandos. It was meant to stop multiple attackers when weapons were not available. Injuries were common in training, even with experienced instructors.

"My. Perhaps you can show me something. Unless you're worried I'll beat you."

Lev smiled. "It will be my pleasure to, ah, show you something."

Nick and Ronnie looked at each other. Nick suppressed a grin.

"After this meeting, then?"

"As you wish."

Elizabeth had watched the exchange, her face betraying nothing of her thoughts. Now she said, "Lev, you'll be staying here, in the guest quarters downstairs. It's quite comfortable. I want you to work with everyone, on the range, in the gym. Just for a few days until we have a mission set up. Give you a chance to get to know one another."

Half an hour later everyone gathered in the gym to watch the match. Lev Gefen had at least fifty pounds on Selena and several inches in reach. Both he and Selena wore loose, black outfits. If Gefen was surprised at the black belt around Selena's waist, he didn't show it. He had one of his own.

"I'll try not to hurt you," he said.

"I appreciate it," Selena said. She smiled.

Nick was acting as referee. "Ready? Remember, don't do any real damage."

Lev and Selena bowed to each other. Gefen attacked. Selena blocked with her arms and tried a leg sweep. Gefen blocked her sweep, countered with his elbow. Selena brushed it aside and half turned. Her leg shot out in a blur, heel extended The blow landed on his upper thigh and knocked him all the way across the mat.

"That would have been your knee," she said.

Gefen's face got red. He attacked again, a flurry of elbow strikes, kicks and punches. Selena blocked and parried, took a body blow, whirled and knocked Gefen's legs out from under him. He went down hard on his back. Selena was on him, her knee resting lightly on his groin, her hand a sharp fist poised high overhead for a killer strike.

"You're dead," she said. She tapped him on the forehead and moved away in a fluid, quick motion. Nick marveled at her agility. It was if she had springs in her legs.

Gefen got to his feet. Nick waited to see how he would handle the ease with which Selena had beaten him. For an Alpha male like Gefen, getting beaten by a woman was probably a new experience. It was the kind of situation that revealed more about who someone was than all the files and training in the world.

He bowed. "I underestimated you," he said. "I apologize if what I said gave offense."

Selena bowed back. "No offense taken."

"Welcome to the team," Harker said.

CHAPTER FORTY-SIX

Phillip Harrison called Croft on a secure link from his Boston office. The view from the office was spectacular. Harrison could look down like Zeus from Olympus on the Charles River and the city. It was a sensation he enjoyed, knowing he was far above the worker ants below. He watched a group of racing sculls cut thin, white lines on the river surface.

"Weisner is gaining ground in the Israeli election but he needs a boost," Harrison said.

"What do you want to do?"

"We implement plan B. Stage an assassination attempt on Weisner. Kill one or two of the people next to him. Don't warn him. That way it will look completely authentic. Make sure you've got a convenient Palestinian patsy handy, someone who's not too smart. We need to do it quickly."

"He's speaking at a big rally in Tel Aviv in two days. It can be arranged. What is the status on the Ark?"

"We have no leads at all. I have people watching the Project people. If there was anything in that tomb, they've got it now. They'll follow up on it and we'll follow them. Then we'll see."

"They've been a real problem."

"Yes, they have. Once we know where the Ark is, we'll eliminate them. In the meantime, we have to be patient."

"Boyd is getting nervous."

"He ought to be. His financial position is overextended. He needs to see the price of crude go up."

"It will go up. As soon as the shooting starts."

"I'll talk to him," Harrison said. "He's in too deep for second thoughts."

"Do you think we'll find it, Phillip?" There was something wistful in Croft's voice.

"You mean the Ark?"

"Yes. Imagine. The real Ark of the Covenant. I wonder if it looks like the pictures and drawings people make of it? The two angels with their wings stretching in, all golden."

"Cherubim, Arthur, not angels."

"What's the difference?"

Harrison didn't feel like giving Croft a rundown on the hierarchy of angels. "When we find it, it won't matter."

"Do you think it had any real, mystical power?"

Yes, but I'm not going to tell you that, Harrison thought. "Only what people gave it," he said.

After he'd hung up, Harrison thought about the Ark. When it was in his possession he would use it to sweep away the non-believers. He would use it to motivate a new crusade. The Holy Land would be safe again.

God would surely be pleased.

CHAPTER FORTY-SEVEN

The team and Lev Gefen sat in Elizabeth's office.
Stephanie had brought in flowers from the garden, a touch of
fresh color on Harker's desk. An East Coast summer simmered
outside, humid and hot. Inside the office, it was pleasant and
comfortable.

"I've been thinking about the coat of arms on that pouch
we found in the church," Selena said.

"What about it?" Elizabeth said.

"The crest shows ten birds around the edge of the shield,
with horizontal stripes. I looked it up. That's the crest of the de
Valence family, William and Aymer, the 1st and 2nd Earls of
Pembroke. William died in 1296, Aymer in 1324."

"That was the 1st Earl of Pembroke's tomb we opened,"
Nick said. "Makes sense the pouch would have his crest."

"Except that isn't his crest. There's more than one 1st Earl
of Pembroke."

"How can there be more than one?" Ronnie asked. He had
on one of his Hawaiian shirts, a red and white pattern of
impossible flowers glowing with almost psychedelic intensity.

"The title goes with the estates, handed out by the King or
Queen. It keeps going until that line dies out. When a new
family takes over, the numbering starts again. William Marshal
died in 1219. Almost eighty years before William de Valence
held the title."

"Then what's the other guy's crest doing there?" Ronnie
said.

"That's what I've been asking myself. We need to make
some assumptions based on what we know so far."

"Go on," Elizabeth said.

"De Molay sends the Ark and maybe the Templar treasure
to England, so the Templar Commander can hide it. That's la

More. La More is tortured and dies, but doesn't reveal where it is. La More is the one who placed the letter in the tomb. That's assumption number one."

"That seems logical."

"Number two is that there's a good reason to use that pouch to hold the letter, with that crest."

"Okay."

"Why put it in the tomb?" she asked.

"To hide it," Nick said.

Gefen watched the exchange. It was the first time he'd seen how everyone worked together. How they figured things out.

"Of course. But why does it have that coat of arms on it? It's not la More's. It doesn't belong to the man buried in the tomb. Why a crest at all? A coat of arms was a message. It told you who the person was, their heritage. It was a medieval ID for all to see."

"For the big shots," Ronnie said.

"That's right. Peasants didn't have crests, only nobility."

"I think I see where you're going," Nick said. "You think the crest is a message."

"Yes. A clue to where the Ark was hidden."

"What do you think it means?"

"I don't know. Something about the Earls of Pembroke, but not William Marshall. De Valence."

"De Valence was alive when de Molay wrote that letter?"

"The father was dead. The son was alive."

"Was the son a Templar?" Lev asked. It was the first thing he'd said.

"I don't think so," Selena said. "If he was known to be a Templar he would have been arrested."

"So why point in the direction of de Valence?" Nick said.

"Say that again, what you just said."

"Why point in the direction of..."

"That's it!" Selena said. She was excited. "The crest is meant to point you at de Valence."

"This is all speculation," Gefen said. "How can you make a plan based on this?"

"It's all we've had from the start," Elizabeth said, "speculation. It's got us this far."

Ronnie cracked his knuckles. "What do the guy in the tomb and de Valence have in common?"

"They both held the title of Earl of Pembroke," Selena said.

"What else?"

"They held the same estates. The main castle still exists. It's in Scotland."

"Scotland might be a good place to stash something you didn't want anyone to find."

"You think the Ark is in Scotland?" Lev felt completely confused.

"Maybe we should take a closer look at that castle," Ronnie said.

"No problem." Stephanie had her laptop. It was hooked into the Crays and the monitor on Harker's wall. The monitor lit. She entered a search for Pembroke Castle.

"Lots of links." She clicked on one. An article and picture came up on the screen.

"Big castle," Ronnie said.

The castle had high ramparts of stone, a tower keep and walls 20 feet thick. It sat on land that stuck out like a thumb into the Pembroke River in West Wales. Three sides were surrounded by the river. The fourth side had a thick wall, a gate and tower. Beyond the castle was the town of Pembroke.

They read the article. "The place was mostly restored in the last century," Nick said. "If something was hidden there, wouldn't they have found it?"

"Not necessarily," Stephanie said. She clicked on a different link. "Here's something interesting. The castle is built over a limestone cavern carved out by water erosion. The Earls used it for storage. It's called Wogan Cavern."

A picture of the cave appeared on the screen.

"Caves are good places to hide something," he said, "but if anything was there, it's long gone."

"Sometimes there's more than one cave in a limestone formation like that," Selena said. "There could be connecting caves. If there are, something could be hidden in them."

"I'll task a satellite for a deep scan," Elizabeth said. "If there's another cave it will show up."

CHAPTER FORTY-EIGHT

Nick took Lev Gefen to the part of the old Nike site that had been converted into a shooting range and armory. He entered a code on a wall mounted keypad. Panels slid back to reveal a full array of personal assault weapons. They all had one thing in common; deadly efficiency.

Lev looked at the racks of weapons. "Interesting," he said. He took an MP-5 from it's place, checked to see if it was loaded, held it to his shoulder. "I always liked these. We use the Tavor C21."

"That's a fine weapon in the field," Nick said. "We mostly use the MP-5s and the SIG-Sauer. We've switched over to .40 Smith and Wesson. Makes it easy to keep the ammo straight."

"A good round. That is what we use in our pistols. What you call a Baby Eagle."

"The Jericho 941."

Lev nodded.

"Pick a pistol. I take it you didn't bring yours."

"No. Ari told me you would take care of it."

Lev took a Sig-Sauer P229 from the rack. All the pistols were flat black. No stainless styling to catch a stray ray of light and give away a position. "This will do."

Nick nodded. "The 226 is a little more accurate, but these are easier to carry. Let's practice."

Nick ran man-sized silhouette targets out to the end of the shooting lanes. They loaded up, put on glasses and ear protection and began firing. After a half hour, they stopped.

"Nice shooting, Lev."

The Israeli's targets were consistent. Tight groups centered on the body. Occasional two shot groups to the head, for variety. Gefen could shoot. Nick hoped he didn't have to find out if the Israeli could do the same thing when the targets were shooting back.

There was a meeting with Harker and the rest of the team in half an hour. They began cleaning the guns.

"Your file says you're married."

"That's right. My wife's name is Rachel. We've got two children."

Lev ran a cleaning brush through the bore of his pistol. The distinctive smell of Hoppe's No. 9 filled the room. He set the pistol down and took out his wallet. He showed Nick pictures.

"This is Aaron. He's five. And this is Rebecca. She's seven."

The children were laughing, splashing each other in a backyard pool. "Rebecca thinks she's the boss, but Aaron always gets even. They're good kids. This is Rachel."

His wife was dark haired, with strong features and a wide smile.

"You're a lucky man, Lev." For just an instant, Nick wondered what it would be like to have children. Megan had wanted children. He thought of Megan and pushed the image away. Megan was gone, a long time ago. Now he was with Selena. She hadn't brought up the subject of children and neither had he. Sometimes it was best to let things be.

Gefen put the pictures away, picked up the gun and began running patches through the barrel. He kept changing them until they came out clean.

"How about you, Nick? You are with Selena, no?"

"You could say that." Nick looked at his watch. "Let's finish up. Time to get upstairs."

There was something in his voice. Lev decided not to pursue it.

Harker had satellite images up on the big screen when they entered her office. Ronnie and Selena and Stephanie were already there.

"Glad you could join us," Elizabeth said.

"Sorry." They sat down.

"This was taken yesterday," she said. "It's a deep infrared scan of Pembroke castle. You can see the difference between the castle walls and buildings and the underlying cavern. The structures on the surface are warmer, so they're very distinct. The darker space underneath on the river side is the cavern. Look at the end away from the river."

The shape of the cavern was a large, oblong egg under the castle grounds. There was a smaller shape on one side, with a thin line signaling a different heat gradient between it and the larger cavern. There was another vague heat differential within the smaller space.

"It's another cave," Nick said, "sealed off from the big one."

"It looks like there's something inside it," Ronnie said. "Those different gradients."

"The barrier isn't very thick. You should be able to break it down without too much trouble. Set it up, Nick," Harker said. "We have to know if the Ark is in that cave. Whatever you do, don't get caught. We don't need another international incident."

"How soon do you want us to go?"

Harker picked up her pen. "Yesterday would be good."

CHAPTER FORTY-NINE

The Welsh village of Pembroke was dominated by the 12th Century castle. The main street of the town was lined with two and three story houses with steeply pitched roofs, laid out along a stretch of quiet water called the Mill Pond. The houses were painted in faded pastel colors, green and lavender, yellow and red. The town had the feel of an aging pensioner about it, as if time had started to leave it behind.

They checked into the Royal George Hotel, not far from the castle, on the pond side of the town. It had a pub that looked inviting. Their rooms were comfortable, in the way of small European hotels that provide a personal touch.

The clerk recommended they take the Mill Pond Walk and handed them a map of the town and castle.

"Castle's closing tomorrow for repairs, I'm afraid," he said. "You still have time for a tour, if you hurry."

Outside the hotel they looked up at the massive walls of the castle.

"How would you like to try and get through that with a sword?" Ronnie said.

The castle would have presented real problems for a 13th Century attacker. The walls were thick and high, built of strong Welsh stone. Rounded towers with battlements marched along the fortifications. The wall facing the town featured a heavily reinforced gatehouse.

Selena read from the guide book. "That kind of gate was called a Barbican. It says they stopped using them a century or so after the castle was built."

"You can see why they used catapults and rams," Lev said. "Even then, it would take serious men to breach those walls."

"You'd be climbing ladders with pots of burning oil and arrows raining down on your head," Selena said. "If you managed to reach the ramparts, you'd face a wall of swords and spears. All hand to hand."

"Books make it sound romantic," Nick said. "But it's still the same old story. Blood and death with the flags waving."

Lev nodded agreement. "It hasn't changed much. We're just more efficient, now. One flight of F-16s would make this whole thing go away."

"You're a cynic, Lev."

"No. A realist. I hate war. I've lived with it my entire life."

They paid the admission fee and entered the castle grounds and found themselves in the Outer Ward, the first defended area. Across the way was a tall stone tower called the Great Keep. It dominated the castle grounds. From the top of the tower, defenders could have seen the entire force attacking them. They would have retreated to the Keep for a last stand, if the outer walls were breached by an attack.

Wogan Cavern was at the bottom of a long, winding staircase of stone that began in a building called the North Hall, on the river side of the compound. They descended single file down the narrow stairs and into the cavern. A half dozen tourists milled about, taking pictures.

The cave was about 80 feet long by 60 wide. The roof was high overhead. The limestone walls were moist, the floor uneven with small puddles of water in the hollows.

The open end of the cavern faced out onto the river. Two tall, narrow windows with iron grills were set above and to the right of a wide, arched opening closed off by a gate of black iron bars. Late afternoon sunlight streamed through the openings. It was like stepping back in time a thousand years. Nick half expected men with swords and hard looks to come down those winding stairs and ask them what they were doing there.

Selena consulted her tourist guide.

"It says the gate was probably used to launch boats down to the river."

"That's our way in later," Nick said. "Let's look for that cave."

They walked to the wall where the satellite had shown a second cave. It looked exactly like the other walls.

"I don't see anything," Lev said.

"There has to be something. Look harder."

"Here," Selena said. She ran her fingers over the surface.

They stood next to her and peered at the surface of the wall. There was a faint line in the irregular stone, so faint no one would see it if they weren't looking in the right spot. The passage of centuries and the constant drip of moisture had blended the marks of the opening into the ridges and valleys of the walls. Nick had to look twice to be sure.

"Have to hand it to them," Ronnie said. "You really can't tell."

"Let's check out the gate," Nick said.

The gate was strong and locked, but the weakness of any gate was in the lock.

"It won't take long to get through it," Ronnie said.

The land sloped away from the gate down to the river.

"We could get right to it from the water."

"How are we going to get the Ark out of there?" Lev said. "Assuming it's behind that wall?"

"Carry it. We need a boat big enough."

"And then?"

"We'll load it in the van. Then we go to the nearest US air base. Probably Fairford in Gloucestershire. Then we get a lift back to the States."

"Maybe it should go to Tel Aviv."

"We'll decide that when and if we find it," Nick said.

"Too bad Lamont isn't here," Selena said. "Water, boats, a night mission. It's what he loves."

Lev said nothing.

"We've seen enough," Nick said. "Let's head back into town and find out about boats. We'll go tomorrow night."

They started the steep climb back to the castle hall above.
Behind them, a man wearing a light windbreaker followed. At
the top, he paused and watched them walk away toward the
gatehouse. He took out his phone and pressed a number.

"Yes."

"I think they've discovered something."

"You know what to do."

"It could get messy."

"If they find something, take it and eliminate them.
Minimize any collateral damage. And make damn sure you
don't get caught."

"Yes, sir."

The man in the windbreaker turned off his phone. He
glanced at his watch. The others should have arrived by now.
They'd be waiting for him back in town.

CHAPTER FIFTY

The Conference Center at the Dan Panorama Hotel in Tel Aviv was packed. Ari Herzog stood near the back of the room and eyed the crowd. On stage, Joshua Weisner was railing about the policies of the current government. The man could speak, Ari gave him that, but the longer he listened, the more his head hurt. One thing Ari knew for certain was that there was no easy solution to what was usually called the Palestinian Problem. He considered rabble rousers like Weisner part of that problem. For Ari, Weisner's so-called solutions were a recipe for disaster and perpetual war.

Agents of Shin Bet were scattered throughout the Center. Herzog monitored their murmured comments through his earpiece. A riot had started the last time this man had addressed a large crowd like this, with forty people ending up in the hospital. Herzog wished people like Weisner would just go away. But they weren't going to go away until there was peace, which seemed farther off to Herzog than it had ever been.

Weisner had just finished describing the need for more settlements on the West Bank when the first shot rang out, the deep bark of a large caliber rifle. An aide crumpled forward onto the stage. The second shot took out a security guard rising to his feet. Weisner ducked down behind the podium. People began screaming.

Herzog yelled into his mike. "In the back! The shooter is in the back!"

He drew his pistol and turned in time to see the third shot fired. A man with a rifle stood at the back of the room. One of Ari's agents lay unmoving at the man's feet.

Ari fired. The Jericho was an accurate weapon as far as side arms went, but the range wasn't good. He missed. The man swung the rifle in his direction. Ari ran toward him and fired again, three shots, then three more. Screams filled the room. People tripped over chairs and trampled each other as they tried to scramble out of the way.

Some of Ari's bullets went home. The man staggered and the rifle fired. A woman dressed in a gold evening gown was blown backward by the round. Ari fired again. He kept firing until the slide locked. The shooter jerked spasmodically as the rounds struck and fell back to the floor. Ari ejected the empty magazine and inserted another as he reached the rifleman. His agents were converging on the body. The shooter lay on the floor, blood pooling around him.

"Call the ambulances," Ari shouted. "Lock down the hotel. Now! And keep people away from this man."

He looked down at the body. How the hell did he get past security with that rifle? It was a question a lot of people would be asking. Another was who the shooter was and where he'd come from. Maybe he was Palestinian. Maybe he wasn't. That was part of the problem. Jews and Arabs often looked the same. They carried the same genes. They just didn't believe in the same things.

One of his agents came up to him.

"Ambulances on the way. The hotel's being sealed." He paused. "The Broadcasting Authority was live on the air."

Damn, Ari thought. This was a key election event. Practically everyone in the nation would have been watching on television. Weisner's stock would rise to the stratosphere. He'd be seen as a champion, an almost martyr to the security of Israel. The election had just gotten a lot closer.

Ari prodded the body with his toe. "Get this piece of crap to the morgue. Find out who he is. If he's Hezbollah or one of the other groups, there's going to be big trouble."

"What about Weisner?"

Ari looked at the stage. Joshua Weisner was gone, hustled away by his security detail.

"What about him?"

"Do you want to talk to him? He's backstage."

"No," Ari said. "I've heard enough talk from him for one day."

CHAPTER FIFTY-ONE

"Someone tried to assassinate Joshua Weisner last night," Harker said. "Israel is on high alert."

Nick was in his room at the George Hotel. The secure satellite connection was good.

"Is there ever a time when they aren't? Who did it?"

"A Palestinian. They've ID'd him as Hezbollah. There are large, organized demonstrations in Lebanon, people shooting into the air, flag burnings, lots of martyr rhetoric. You know the drill."

"How is the government reacting?"

"They have to appear strong. Prime Minister Lerner has been forced into a corner. If he doesn't retaliate, he'll be seen as weak right before an election. If he does retaliate, there'll be diplomatic outbursts, world condemnation, riots. The usual. It's a Catch-22. A lot depends on exactly what he does."

"What's your best guess?" Nick asked.

"Our satellites show massive preparations. Troops mobilizing, planes being fueled, the whole nine yards. Lerner is a conservative moderate and a staunch supporter of Israel's security. He and everyone else is fed up with Hezbollah. My guess is that he's going to invade Lebanon and go after them. He'd gain the backing of the extreme conservative elements right before the election. It means a blood bath, with lots of civilian casualties."

"That didn't work the last time. And Hezbollah is backed by Iran."

"What's different this time is that I think Lerner really means it."

"Hezbollah is backed by Iran."

"That's a problem. I don't think the Mullahs will stand by and let their puppets be taken out of the game."

"Another war?"

"Yes. I hope I'm wrong, but my intuition says otherwise."

Nick sighed. Elizabeth's intuition was usually right on.

"What's your operational status?" Harker asked.

"There's a bright moon tonight, but weather says considerable cloud cover. We'll get in through the river gate, open up that cave and see what we find. There's minimum security at the castle. They don't need it. Once they lock up for the night, it's pretty hard to get in. That was the idea when they built it 900 years ago and nothing has changed. Won't be much of a problem for us, though."

"How's Lev working out?"

"Nothing's happened yet. I expect he'll be fine."

"The problems at home may distract him."

"I'll deal with it."

"All right, Nick. Brief me as soon as you know what's in that cave."

"Roger that."

CHAPTER FIFTY-TWO

The river was calm and black and smelled of green weeds and rushes and mud. A chorus of frogs croaked in chaotic rhythm in the night. The sky was clouded over, the moon a dull glow when it could be seen at all. It was a night that almost defined the words *black ops*.

They'd found a wide, flat-bottomed skiff, big enough to hold them and anything they might discover in the castle. They'd changed into black clothes. Ronnie carried a small pack with the things they needed.

Nick worked the oars, breaking the surface of the river with quiet splashes. Selena watched the towering castle wall draw closer, a darker shape in the blackness of the night.

This is real, she thought. *I'm about to sneak into a 12th Century castle in Britain to look for the Ark of the Covenant.* She felt the adrenaline rush begin, the excitement.

The boat grounded with a soft scrape at the bottom of the slope below Wogan Cavern. They scrambled out. Nick pulled the skiff up out of the water. They climbed up to the gate leading into the cave and Ronnie took out his pouch of tricks. He bent to the lock. A minute later the gate swung open, the hinges making a brief, harsh noise in the night.

Inside the cavern, Nick turned on his light. The LEDs cast an intense, blue-white beam on the limestone walls. They glistened in the cold light. The cavern seemed vast in the darkness. It was silent except for the sound of their breathing and a slow drip of water.

They went to the spot they'd found the day before. Ronnie took a spray can from his pack.

"Better move back," he said. "Makes a lot of fumes."

Ronnie sprayed the contents of the can back and forth across the concealed opening and stepped away. Thick, bitter smoke roiled off the surface. After five minutes, the reaction stopped.

"Now what?" Lev said.

For answer, Ronnie stepped forward. He kicked the wall. It fell inward, revealing a dark opening. A whiff of old, stale air pushed past them.

"Technology is a wonderful thing," he said. "Better living through chemistry."

"We don't have anything like that," Lev said. There was admiration in his voice.

They bent low to enter. Inside, the roof was high enough to stand. Nick moved his light back and forth. The cave was about fifteen feet long and as wide again. Something gleamed white in the back corner. Nick played his light over it. It was a skeleton, wearing a leather tunic and boots and fragments of clothing. A long sword lay at its side. The skull had been cleaved open by a savage blow. The rest of the cave was empty except for rubble on the floor.

"Damn." Nick swore under his breath.

Selena felt a wave of disappointment. There was no Ark. No Templar treasure. Just old bones and debris.

"I wonder what happened to this guy?" Ronnie walked over to the bones. He picked up the sword, swung it across, back again. The blade was over three feet long. It made a thick, deadly sound as it cut through the air.

"Nasty. I wouldn't want to get cut with one of these."

"Can I see that, Ronnie?"

He handed the sword to Selena. She examined the hilt.

"This isn't a 13th Century sword," she said. "Look at the hilt. It's a basket hilt. See the rounded guard and the way the hilt is pierced and sculpted? The earlier swords had wide, heavy blades meant for slashing. This one is narrow, made to thrust. This is from the 17th Century, maybe around the time of Cromwell. It's the right style."

Ronnie was no longer surprised at the things Selena knew. "Who was Cromwell?" he asked.

"A Protestant commander who defeated the Catholic Royalists in England's Civil War. He took over the rule of England. Cromwell is one of the most controversial figures in English history."

"Was he ever here, at Pembroke?"

"I don't know."

Selena played her light over the floor in the center of the cave.

"There was something heavy here," she said. "You can see where it made marks as it was dragged away. A chest, something like that."

"Could it have been the Ark?"

"Maybe. The Ark took four priests to carry it."

Her light caught something shiny on the floor. She bent down and picked it up.

"Gold," she said. "It's a small piece of thin gold. It could have come from the covering of the Ark."

"Looks like we're a few hundred years too late," Nick said. "Let's get out of here. Ronnie, take the sword with you. It's the only connection to whatever happened here."

They went back out to the cavern and through the gate. Nick closed it behind them. The next time someone went into Wogan Cavern, they were in for a surprise.

There was a sound from the river that shouldn't have been there. A boot, scraping on rock.

They dropped flat to the sloping ground. Clothing whispered as they drew their pistols.

Then the night lit with the flash of guns.

CHAPTER FIFTY-THREE

It was late at night in Washington. Elizabeth had just gotten home. She took off her shoes and put her holstered pistol on the counter. She made a cup of chamomile tea and stood at the kitchen counter, thinking about another stressful day.

The sound of the doorbell jolted her. She looked at the monitor and saw a man in a dark suit and tie standing outside. He wore an earpiece. Behind him, a black Lincoln idled in the street.

"Yes." She spoke into the intercom. The man held up an ID to the camera over the door.

"Secret Service, Director. The President would like to see you."

"One moment."

It was unusual for Rice to send a car unannounced. Good thing she hadn't undressed yet. She slipped her shoes back on. She clipped the holster back on her waist. She'd have to hand it over when she got to the White House, but she never went anywhere without it. Even at home, it was never far away.

This time of night, the drive to the White House didn't take very long. She got out at a side entrance. She handed over her gun and was given a visitor badge and followed an agent to the Oval Office.

President James Rice was seated behind his desk, writing something.

"Sir, Director Harker is here."

"Thank you, Bill. Come in, Director."

"Mister President."

"Take a seat, Director." Rice's manner was cool. *Still mad about Jordan,* she thought. *Maybe I'm here to get fired.* The

President looked tired. He always looked tired these last months. Tonight he seemed even more so than usual. His skin had an unhealthy grayish tinge. The black that had been in his hair when he was first elected was completely gone. Rice had aged years since he'd taken office.

"Give me your assessment on Israel," he said. No pleasantries or small talk. Elizabeth gathered her thoughts.

"Sir, I believe Prime Minister Lerner is going to take harsh retaliatory action."

"Go on."

"Lerner loathes Weisner, but this attempted assassination has taken the lid off an old problem."

"You mean Hezbollah."

"Yes, sir. It's highly charged, in a political sense. With the election coming up, Lerner has to act. He can't just send in a strike against a few leaders. That only gets everyone worked up. If I'm reading the situation correctly, he will make an all out effort to remove Hezbollah once and for all."

"That would be unfortunate."

"Yes, sir."

Rice rose. Elizabeth started to get up but he waved her back into her chair. "Don't get up, Elizabeth."

Back to Elizabeth. She breathed an inward sigh of relief. Rice's opinion mattered to her. It wasn't just that he was the Big Boss, or that she operated at his pleasure. She liked him. He had the worst job in the world.

Rice put his hands behind his back and began pacing back and forth. "The Secretary of State doesn't agree with you. She thinks Lerner will follow the usual pattern. Send in an air strike, kill a few militants and maybe some civilians and make the point that you can't try assassination attempts in Israel and get away with it. Defense agrees with her. He says Hezbollah will retaliate with some suicide bombings, fire some rockets and that will be that."

"With all due respect, Mister President, I think they're wrong. Weisner now has at least a 50/50 chance of winning the election. He's got the conservative parties and all of the religious right behind him. Lerner's coalition is falling apart. It already was, or he wouldn't have called an early election like he did. The attack makes it look like the Islamists think Weisner is a serious threat. That translates into votes. If Weisner is elected, any hope of a peace settlement goes out the window."

"And you think Lerner will get tough to prove he's not going to take it anymore."

"Yes, sir. The Israelis are also mobilizing along the West Bank. I think Lerner is going to go after Hamas at the same time. Hezbollah is Iran's major surrogate. Hamas is Sunni, but Iran likes the trouble they cause. If Israel neutralizes those groups it will set back Tehran's plans for an Islamic Middle East by years. They can't let that happen."

"I'm afraid I agree with you."

She paused. "There's something else I'm looking at."

"Yes?"

"I've received highly reliable intelligence from Israel about the shooter. He was nobody, a gofer in Hezbollah, the sort of person they use for menial tasks. Not very smart. It seems odd to me he would be given an important mission like that."

Rice stopped pacing and looked at her. "Are you saying you think this wasn't a genuine attempt? That the shooter was a patsy?"

If she said yes and she was wrong, she'd lose whatever credibility she had left. It didn't matter what her successes had been in the past. The nature of political realities at this level meant mistakes could not be overlooked. Whatever she told Rice would have consequences, for her and for the Nation.

Elizabeth took a breath. "Yes, sir. I think it's a set up. Someone wants to push Israel into another war and they want Weisner as the new PM. If they'd really wanted to kill him, he'd be dead."

"If it wasn't Hezbollah, who was it?"

"I don't know, yet. I'm working on it."

186

"Iran is mobilizing."

"Yes, sir. I saw the satellite intel."

"The last war was barely stopped before it went nuclear." Rice paused, considering what he was about to say. "Langley thinks Iran may have a nuke."

Elizabeth was stunned. She had no knowledge of an Iranian nuke. She had seen nothing to indicate Tehran had succeeded in building a weapon.

"How could they have built a bomb?" she said.

"They didn't. CIA thinks they've gotten hold of a Russian warhead built in the 80s. It was designed for an SS-13 missile but could be modified to fit the Shahab 3. That missile could hit Tel Aviv or Haifa."

"Do the Israelis know this?"

"They do not, nor am I going to tell them just yet. It would lead to rash actions on their part."

"You mean a preemptive strike against Iran."

"They are certain to react in that way."

"Sir, that is a disaster. The Mullahs are unstable. If they have a nuke and it looks like Israel is going to drive Hezbollah from Lebanon, they'll use it. Israel would retaliate with their own nukes."

"Exactly. We are currently at DEFCON 3. If Lerner invades Lebanon, I will go to DEFCON 2. If it looks like Iran is getting ready to launch a strike, I will inform the Israelis of what we've learned."

"Sir, I am sure he is serious."

"I don't like the way this is headed. There's too much risk of a nuclear war. I might be able to stop Lerner if I can show him Hezbollah is not behind this attack on Weisner. You say the assassin was a patsy. Prove it, Elizabeth."

"I'll do my best, Mister President."

"Do it quickly, Director. I don't think there's much time left."

CHAPTER FIFTY-FOUR

Lying there on the steep slope under the castle walls with the whine of bullets passing overhead, Selena entered the zone.

Time turned into a slow motion dream. A light breeze off the water brought the dank, moist smell of the river water and the rushes on the banks, mixed with the sharp odor of burnt gunpowder. She watched the bright, winking flashes of the guns on the river. She fired back at them, watched her pistol rise with the recoil of each shot.

Ronnie lay next to her. She registered the slide on his pistol working back and forth, the empty cases drifting through the air, settling and bouncing around them. Somewhere in the back of her mind she realized they were in a full blown firefight. The sound of the guns seemed far off, muffled. There was another sound. With a shock, she realized she was yelling, an inarticulate scream of primal rage and fear. It snapped the spell. Time sped up again.

They lay on the ground, facing down at the river, everyone firing at the flashes in the water. It sounded like someone had started World War Three.

Then it was over. They waited. Across the water a light came on in someone's house. Then another. There were no more shots from below. Nick risked a quick light. Crumpled shapes lay on the slope below. His beam landed on a boat drifting away from the shore. An arm draped over the edge trailed in the river current. The boat was beginning to settle as water poured through bullet holes in the side. Nick stood. The others got to their feet. All except Lev.

"Lev," Nick said. "Are you all right?"

He bent over the Israeli. Lev lay face down on the ground. The back of his skull was bloody. Brain matter oozed from the wound. Nick rolled him over. There was a large, open wound in his forehead. His eyes were open.

"Shit," Nick said. More lights were going on across the way. "Ronnie, Selena. Help me get him into the boat."

They carried Lev down to the boat. Ronnie ran back up, retrieved the sword and Lev's pistol and got in with the others. They pushed off from shore. Nick rowed hard, back to where they had left the van. Ronnie jumped out, waded to the shore and pulled the skiff in. They picked up Lev's body and put it in the back of the van. They got in the van and headed southeast, back toward England.

Nobody spoke. As Nick drove, he remembered Lev showing him the pictures of his wife and children.

CHAPTER FIFTY-FIVE

Phillip Harrison III leaned back in the comfortable chair in his Boston office and worked to control his anger. The damage was done. Getting angry wouldn't help or fix things. Interference by the Project meant changes had to be made. It was annoying to deal with.

First they had eliminated Anderson, a man he'd relied on for years. It was inconvenient to lose such a valuable resource. Harrison had other sources inside Langley, though none were field agents. Good for gathering intelligence, useless for more difficult kinds of work. Anderson had been good at that. The way he'd dispatched that French mob boss and cleaned up afterward was a perfect example.

Then there was the mercenary he'd contracted with, the man who was supposed to handle things in England. He was dead too, along with his men. Another failure, but also a potential source of exposure eliminated.

Harrison was about to interview a replacement, a man named Nigel McKenzie. He came highly praised by Arthur Croft. The arms merchant said he was ruthless and reliable. It was a solid recommendation.

McKenzie had been an officer in British Special Forces before an incident in Iraq had forced him to resign his commission. Now he ran MKTA Security, a company that provided services to a small number of wealthy clients. McKenzie's employees joked that MKTA stood for Must Kill Them All. If you had trouble with unruly locals at your mines in Africa or South America, or needed someone to discourage the people who wanted to steal your oil, you called MKTA. Once they arrived on the scene, problems quickly ceased.

Harrison wasn't sure what had happened at Pembroke. No one had survived to report back. He didn't think the Project people had found anything, or he would have heard something through his connections in the intelligence community. That meant the Ark was still out there somewhere and that the Project would continue looking for it. He simply had to follow them until they found it. He had contacted McKenzie because he needed someone to finish the job the others had failed to accomplish, and make sure none of the Project personnel were left alive to talk about it afterward. Harrison didn't like to lose. The Project had blocked him at each step of the way. It had become personal.

His secretary came into the office. "Colonel McKenzie is here, sir."

"Send him in."

McKenzie didn't so much as enter the room as fill it with his presence. He was about five ten, a solid, wide man, with shoulders like a bull. His face was hard and brown and dry from years spent under open skies and tropical suns. He moved with contained violence that smoldered behind blue eyes cold as a glacial lake.

Harrison liked him on sight.

"Please, sit down, Colonel."

McKenzie sat. "Nice office." He looked out at the panoramic view of Boston.

"Care for a drink?" Harrison said.

"After we talk, perhaps. Croft said you had an interesting proposition."

McKenzie's voice was thick with an echo of Scotland.

"Colonel, do you know who I am?"

"Enough. I know you are a wealthy man. I know you are having trouble with some, mm, discreet operatives of your government."

"That is correct. They are members of a small intelligence unit."

"What sort of trouble are they making for you?"

"Arthur said I could trust to your discretion. Is that true, Colonel?"

"Please do not insult my intelligence, Mister Harrison."

"Of course, I apologize. I am seeking an object of some antiquity. These people are also looking for it. They have managed to stay ahead of me so far and have also eliminated several valuable assets of mine."

"Ah."

"To be plain, Colonel, I want them eliminated in turn. And I want that object, if they manage to find it."

"You want me to terminate them?"

"That is correct."

"It will be expensive."

"As you said, I am a wealthy man. As long as you propose a reasonable price, there will be no problem."

"I'll need specifics. Who they are, who they work for, where they live. All that."

Harrison slid a folder across his desk. "All in there."

McKenzie nodded. He appreciated efficiency.

"What is this object?"

"Does it matter?"

McKenzie grinned. "Not really. The fee is two million Euros. Half now, half on completion to your satisfaction. One million Euros as a bonus if I secure this...object for you."

"You have considerable faith in your ability," Harrison said. "You understand, failure is not an option."

McKenzie smiled.

"Agreed," Harrison said.

McKenzie took out a pocket notebook and wrote down an account number from a bank in the Caymans. Harrison took the paper and looked at the name of the bank.

"An excellent choice. They are quite secure."

Harrison had a computer monitor on his desk. He pulled a keyboard out and entered a string of commands. He turned the monitor so McKenzie could see it. Then he pressed send.

1,000,000 Euros was transferred from one account to the other.

"I think I'll have that drink now," McKenzie said.

After the man had left, Harrison thought about the meeting. He considered the money well spent, if it brought results. Now that he'd taken steps to get things back on track he could relax a bit.

At least the operation in Israel had gone as planned. Weisner had moved ahead of the Prime Minister in the polls. Harrison didn't really care who won the election. He'd achieved his goal, to provoke a visceral response on both sides of the Middle East equation. War was inevitable, whether the Ark was found or not.

If the Project located the Ark, McKenzie would take it from them. Harrison prayed every day that they would find it. Whether they found it or not, they would soon cease to be a problem.

CHAPTER FIFTY-SIX

Lamont looked like someone had added a little too much cream to the coffee color of his skin. A clear tube fed oxygen to his nostrils. But he was out of danger.

Nick finished telling him about Lev Gefen and the firefight at the castle.

"He had kids? That's a damn shame." Lamont's voice was weak. His breathing was labored. A monitor beeped quietly in the corner of the room.

Nick nodded. "I liked him. He reminded me a little of Korov, that same kind of attitude."

"What happens next?

"Selena is checking on the sword we found. Maybe it leads somewhere. If not, we don't have any other places to look. We're done."

"How are you and her getting along? Before I got hurt, seemed there was some tension between you."

"You picked up on that?"

Lamont laughed. It turned into a fit of coughing. Nick held a cup of water with a straw to his lips.

"You're kidding. Hell, Nick, you two are really obvious. We all know when something's going on."

Nick looked out the window.

"Ronnie said you were living apart again."

Nick looked back at his friend. "Yeah. Seems like a good idea right now. I've been tossing around a lot at night. Keeps her awake."

Lamont let that pass. He knew about Nick's nightmares. He also knew Nick had started seeing a shrink. He didn't say anything about it.

"Sometimes I wonder what the hell we're doing together," Nick said. "I don't know what she wants from me."

Lamont was surprised. Nick never talked about Selena, not to him. Not to Ronnie, either, as far as he knew. Nick kept things to himself. They all did. It went with the territory.

"What do you want from her?"

"Damned if I know. We kind of got caught up in everything and one thing led to another. I don't know where it's supposed to go."

Lamont said nothing.

"Anyway," Nick said, "if we get a lead from that sword we'll follow up. Selena found a bit of gold in the cave. She thinks it was part of the covering on the Ark."

Lamont was relieved Nick had changed the subject.

"The Bible says it was covered in gold, doesn't it?"

"Yes."

"You think it might still be around?"

"If it was in the cave when the guy with the sword was killed, that's only a few hundred years ago."

"Might as well be yesterday."

"My guess is that the dead swordsman was killed protecting it. Or trying to steal it, either way."

"Makes sense."

"The question is who took it and what did they do with it. They could have stripped it for the gold."

"I don't know, Nick. I mean it's the Ark. Everyone knows about it, at least everyone Christian or Jewish."

"Or Muslim. But there weren't any Muslims in Pembroke back then."

"I don't think anyone would just destroy it for the gold."

"You have more faith in humanity than I do."

"If you find it, it would help make Gefen's death worth something," Lamont said.

"There's that, I guess. I don't think it would be a lot of comfort to his wife and kids."

CHAPTER FIFTY-SEVEN

It was a day full of sunshine in the New City of Jerusalem, a perfect contrast to Ari Herzog's dark mood. He waited for Rachel Gefen to open the door. He'd brought a woman with him, another Shin Bet agent. He thought it would be good to have a woman along when he told Rachel of her husband's death. Lev had been a friend. Ari and Lev and Rachel had shared good times together. Ari felt that he had to be the one to tell her, but he wasn't looking forward to it.

Rachel opened the door. She was a handsome woman, not exactly beautiful, with strong, square features that spoke of her Polish ancestors. Her hair was her best feature, dark and lustrous, falling to her shoulders.

"Ari." Rachel was surprised. "What brings you here this time of day?"

"Are the children here, Rachel?"

"No, they're in school. Who is this with you?"

Ari looked at his companion. "This is Rebecca."

"Our daughter is named Rebecca." She looked at him. Something passed over her face. The warmth of seeing him went out of it.

"It's Lev. You're here about Lev, aren't you? Why isn't he with you?"

"Rachel..."

"Why isn't he with you?" Her voice rose.

"Can I come in?"

"No. Where's Lev, Ari?"

"I'm sorry, Rachel."

"I won't hear this. I do not want to hear you say you're sorry. Where is Lev?"

There wasn't any way to make it easy. "The *chevra kaddisha* is with him."

The holy society was a group of unpaid volunteers who prepared the body for burial.

Rachel's hand flew to her face. A loud wail came from her throat. Ari stood helpless, unable to do anything for the wife of his friend. Rachel leaned against the door and began sobbing.

"Rachel..." he said.

Rebecca put a hand on his arm. "Let me, Ari." She went to Lev's wife. "Come," she said. "Let's go inside."

Ari watched the door close behind them.

CHAPTER FIFTY-EIGHT

The team studied a live satellite shot from high above Israel. Harker focused on the border with Jordan and Syria, then shifted to the Gaza Strip and Egypt. Everywhere, troops were mobilizing.

"Lerner is going to re-occupy the West Bank," Elizabeth said. "He's staging troops on the border with Lebanon and getting ready to go after Hezbollah."

"Tehran isn't going to let this happen without doing something," Nick said.

"The last time Israel went into Lebanon after Hezbollah it ended in a draw. This time, there's a heavier concentration of troops and logistics. Lerner means to smash them, once and for all."

"It will never work," Selena said. "Even if he succeeds, the militants will just regroup. In another year or two it will be the same old story."

"Maybe not," Elizabeth said. "This time it could go nuclear."

"What do you mean?" Nick said. "Israel doesn't need to use nukes. They didn't last time."

"It's Iran I'm worried about." She told them what Rice had said.

"This is confirmed?" Nick asked.

"Yes. Confirmation came in last night. A 600 Kiloton warhead salvaged from a Russian SS-13 Savage ICBM. It could be modified to fit one of Iran's conventional missiles. They have several that could reach Israel."

"When did they get it?"

"Three weeks ago."

"That could give them enough time to make the modifications."

"Yes. But we don't know the condition of the warhead. It's old. It could be corroded, unstable. They'd have to disassemble and reinstall it. It's not that easy."

"That is really bad news," Ronnie said.

"We can't do anything about it," Harker said, "except what we've been doing. Selena, what have you found out about that sword?"

"It's an officer's sword. Both the Royalists and the Parliamentarians carried swords during the English Civil War, but I think this one belonged to a Royalist. It's a rapier with silver fittings. That's typical."

"Wait a second," Ronnie said. "Who are the Parliamentarians?"

She brushed her hand across her forehead. "The war was between the Protestant Parliamentarians, under Oliver Cromwell, and the Catholic Royalists. The two sides are called the Cavaliers and the Roundheads."

"The Royalists backed the King?" Ronnie said.

"Right. They're the Cavaliers. There was a Royalist revolt at Pembroke Castle, with troops changing sides. Cromwell laid siege to Pembroke in 1648. That's probably when the man with the sword was killed. It has to be when the Ark was removed from the hiding place we found."

"So you think that Cromwell's men found the Ark," Nick said, "because the skeleton we found belongs to a Royalist."

"I think he was killed defending it."

"Then what happened to the Ark?"

"Oliver Cromwell was very serious about his religion, a Puritan. He wouldn't have wanted people worshipping it or making a big fuss over it."

"He could have destroyed it," Elizabeth said.

"I don't think he'd do that," Selena said. "But he could have hidden it."

"Where?"

"Well, that's the question."

"What happened after the siege of Pembroke?" Nick asked.

"Cromwell became Lord Protector of England in 1649. He had the King beheaded. Cromwell died in 1658. His son Richard took over, but he lasted less than a year. Richard went into exile and the monarchy was restored. Eventually he came back to England. He died in Hertfordshire, while staying on a friend's estate."

Harker had begun tapping her pen. "The history is interesting, but I don't see how it helps us."

"We only have assumptions," Selena said. "Guesses. My guess is that the Ark was found by Oliver Cromwell at Pembroke Castle and hidden by him. When the time came, Crowell knew he was dying. I think he would have passed the secret on to his son."

"If he did, the son would have kept a close eye on it," Nick said.

"And hidden it in turn," Ronnie said.

"Where?"

"I need to do some research," Selena said. "If Richard Cromwell hid the ark, there could be some reference in his papers that only makes sense with that idea in mind."

Nick saw the expression on her face. *There's something about research that really turns her on*, he thought.

"How do you plan to get the papers?"

"I can see some of them online, but I'll need to go to England."

"Take Nick and Ronnie with you," Harker said.

CHAPTER FIFTY-NINE

Richard Cromwell had spent his last days on an estate 50 miles northeast of London, near Cambridge University. Most of his letters and papers were in the Cambridgeshire Archives. If there was anything in Cromwell's correspondence that could shed light on the location of the Ark, it would be somewhere in those archives.

They checked into a hotel near the University early in the afternoon of a perfect English summer day, the kind of day that had inspired Shakespeare to compare. From there they went to the County Council record office, where Cromwell's papers were stored. The office was in Shire Hall, a massive building of stone in a style much favored for government buildings at the height of Empire. It projected bureaucratic power.

Selena had already examined the Cromwell letters that could be seen online and discovered nothing. Some of the fragile documents were available only for serious research and only by permission. Selena's academic credentials smoothed the way to the restricted section.

"This is going to take a while," she said. "You and Ronnie don't need to be here."

"We passed a pub down the road. Ronnie and I will go there. Call when you want us to come pick you up."

Three hours later she found what she was looking for. She called Nick and went outside to wait for him.

When they pulled up outside Shire Hall, they appeared unusually happy.

"We found a good pub," Nick said. "Had shepherd's pie for lunch. Good beer, too."

"Better let me drive," she said.

As they drove away from the Council offices, a dark blue Volvo started up in the parking lot and pulled out after them.

"They're headed back into town," the driver said into his radio link.

"Keep your distance. They're probably going back to their hotel."

"What's our next move?"

"We watch and wait. If they turned anything up, they'll go after it. It's getting late. Probably nothing's going to happen until tomorrow. Make sure you've got somebody on them all the time."

"Roger that," the man said.

"Don't screw up."

"Roger," the man said again.

CHAPTER SIXTY

Selena's room had a balcony and a view of Cambridge University's King's College. The chapel bell tower dominated the skyline. Nick and Ronnie sat on a couch in front of a low, glass-topped coffee table. Selena took a chair by the desk.

"Richard Cromwell was forced out of power in 1659," she said. "He went into exile in France in 1660. I found a letter he wrote from France to his daughter, Elizabeth. I think he had the Ark and hid it before he left and she was in on it. In the letter he begins with the usual Puritan thinking, telling her to be mindful of her place before God. Then he talks about his illness and having blood let. Doctors back then would bleed you for just about anything."

"Did it do any good?"

"Not enough. There are some who think his doctors killed him." She paused. "Cromwell was a Puritan. To understand the letter, you have to understand how the Puritans thought about things."

"Tall black hats," Ronnie said. "Blunderbusses. Thanksgiving."

Selena ignored him. "In Puritan society women and men were considered equal in a spiritual sense, but subservient to men in every other way, except with things that concerned the home and raising children. In the home, the women made the decisions."

"Took a while to change that, didn't it?" Ronnie said.

"Who said it's changed? Anyway, Richard appears to have had a great love for his daughter. He treated her in a way somewhat different than you might expect, more as an equal. She was devoted to him as well. In the letter he refers to the English Restoration of 1660. That was when the Anglican

Church was restored to it's former position as the official Church of England."

"You should have been a history professor," Nick said.

"Sorry. The point is that when the Restoration took place, many of the churches that had been Presbyterian or Calvinist under Oliver Cromwell went back to being Anglican. I think Richard hid the Ark in a Presbyterian church when he was forced out of power. That church later became Anglican."

"Do you know which one it is?"

"My best guess is St. John's, near the town of Chesthunt. It's not far from London."

"Why there?"

"Chesthunt is where Richard Cromwell died. He had a wealthy friend there, a merchant named Thomas Pengally. Cromwell stayed on his estate before and after he came back from France. It makes sense that if he had the Ark he'd keep it nearby. The letter refers to '*That whiche is fairre to be tresr'd, nor cast before swine*'. He cautions his daughter to remain silent about it before men and speak of it only to God. I think he means the Ark. In the next sentence he describes the pleasing simplicity of the altar at St. John's. It's an odd thing to put in where he did."

"That which is fair?" Nick said. "He could have been referring to his daughter."

"I don't think so. I think he could have hidden the Ark in that altar."

"Slim."

"It's all we've got and it's not that far away."

She waited.

"Like you say, it's all we've got. We'll go down there tonight and find out."

"I'll see what I can find out about the church online," Selena said.

In the hotel room directly below, a man put down a set of headphones. He turned to another figure standing nearby.

"Got it," the man with the headphones said.

Nigel McKenzie nodded. "Get the men ready."

CHAPTER SIXTY-ONE

Elizabeth was at her desk, reviewing the latest intelligence reports from the Middle East. Burps pawed at her leg.

"I can't tell you what I'm doing. You're not cleared for it. No, I don't have any food for you," Elizabeth said. "Go see Stephanie. Better yet, go outside."

She got up and opened the door to the garden. "Shoo." She pointed.

Burps looked at her. "Mrrow," he said. He looked offended and stalked into the garden. Elizabeth shut the door.

You were talking to a cat, she thought, *telling him he wasn't cleared. This job is getting to you.*

Stephanie came into the room.

"Iran just told Israel not to go into Lebanon," Elizabeth said. "They're ramping up the rhetoric."

"That's predictable."

"Yes. And Lerner is turning into a real hard liner. No more Mister Nice Guy. He really wants to stay on as Prime Minister."

"What did he do now?"

"He warned Tehran that they've reached the limit of Israeli patience. Any overt moves on the part of the Iranians to aid Hezbollah will be considered an act of war."

Stephanie considered that. "What's Rice doing?"

"Pressuring the Iraqi government to deny permission for Iranian over flights. Tehran is beginning to supply Hezbollah from the air."

"Good luck with that," Stephanie said. "That so-called government in Baghdad is another disaster waiting to happen."

"Why Stephanie," Harker said. "How can you be so critical of one of our few democratic friends in the area?"

"With them for friends, we don't need any more enemies."

"Since Iranian flights have already started, I have to agree with you."

"What's Lerner doing about Hezbollah?"

"Getting ready to unleash the IDF on them. Russia and China have called for an emergency meeting of the UN Security Council. The song and dance is starting."

"You're just full of good news today, Elizabeth."

"Actually there is some good news. Selena thinks she's located the Ark. Or at least a possibility of where it might be."

"Which is?"

"In England, in a church. They're going after it tonight."

"I'll believe it when I see it," Stephanie said.

CHAPTER SIXTY-TWO

St. John's was the kind of picturesque English church that found its way onto postcards. It was set in the countryside about a mile from the nearest village. Ronnie parked away from the building, by a graveyard filled with old, tilted monuments and markers. A bright moon cast shadows from the ancient stones.

The church was large, the stone walls gray and solid in the moonlight. The main part of the church was a long rectangle with a peaked roof. A tall, square bell tower rose at the end. An arched vestibule jutted out halfway down the side, flanked by pairs of narrow stone windows with diamond panes. A row of similar windows marched the length of the church along the roof.

The rectory was a separate building set off to the side. A path led to it from the church. The windows of the rectory were dark, the door shut tight against the night.

A pair of arched wooden doors led into the vestibule. The lock looked old, the kind of lock that opened with a heavy iron key. The doors were reinforced with iron straps and black iron hinges. Iron rings were mounted on each door. Ronnie grasped one and gently pulled. The door moved.

"It's not locked," he said.

Nick's ear was itching. "Something doesn't feel right."

"Nobody knows we're here," Selena said. Her voice was quiet. Her heart was pounding. She took a deep breath, another.

"Yeah. Lock and load," Nick said.

The guns came out. Nick nodded and Ronnie pulled the door open.

The vestibule was twelve feet deep and twice again as wide. A closed oak door led from the vestibule to the church.

Nick eased it open and signaled the others to wait. He stepped into the church.

The interior was dim, quiet, lit by moonlight coming through the windows and a pair of fat candles burning on two high brass candleholders at the front. The roof was braced with a tented cross work of thick wooden rafters and beams, all of it supported by massive round columns of stone. From where he stood, the front of the church and the altar was to his left. A tall wooden pulpit reached by a narrow, spiral stair rose on the right of the altar, where the sermon would be read over the heads of the congregation. Behind it was the empty choir.

Marble plaques with the names of men fallen on one of England's many battlefields lined the walls. Rows of plain wooden pews took up both sides of a central aisle. A cross was set on the wall behind the altar.

There was something wrong. It took Nick a moment to realize that the altar was askew. It should have been placed at the end of the nave in the center, parallel to the congregation. But it was crooked, as if it had been moved. It was a solid rectangle of dark wood. There should have been things on it, a cross, candles, but it was bare. A white cloth lay crumpled on the floor beside it.

Nick's ear began to burn. There was a muffled cough from somewhere inside the church.

"Hit the deck!" he yelled.

Nick dove for the floor. Gunfire erupted from behind the altar and the pulpit. The rounds blew sharp splinters out of the door behind him. Automatic weapons opened up from the other end of the building, shattering the pews in front of him. Nick wriggled backward into the vestibule. Shots came from outside the church, thudding into the heavy wooden doors and ricocheting from the stone.

They were pinned down.

CHAPTER SIXTY-THREE

Elizabeth and Stephanie watched a live satellite feed of the war taking shape in the Middle East. The Israeli Defense Force was poised at the border with Lebanon, set for a full blown assault. Naval units were positioned to bombard Sidon on the coast. Troop movements could be seen clearly on the satellite feed. Hezbollah was moving rocket batteries into position. Elizabeth knew they had Iranian missiles hidden somewhere in the hills.

On the West Bank, Israeli troops were already pouring through the checkpoints and pushing hard for the camps. The Arab world was in an uproar. The UN Security Council was in emergency session. There were mass demonstrations in Iran, Syria, Lebanon and Egypt.

"I think Lerner will go all the way to Beirut," Elizabeth said. "He'll secure the south below Sidon first. That will eliminate the rocket bases. Then he'll try to force a settlement that drives Hezbollah out of the country. On the West Bank, he's going for the '67 cease fire line."

"The border with Jordan. What's Syria doing?"

"Making a lot of noise, mostly. They're still enmeshed in their civil war. There isn't much they can do."

She picked up her pen, set it down. "Rice has put the subs on DEFCON2 and held everyone else for the moment at DEFCON3. He doesn't want to send the wrong signals, but he's worried. Russia and China have raised their alert levels as well. If someone makes a mistake it could go out of control fast."

"What about that Iranian nuke?"

"That's the wild card. We don't know where it is, or what they're planning. We don't have a lot of assets in Iran. They've gotten first-class at counter-intelligence and they don't like spies."

The cat was outside, pawing at the garden door.

"Burps wants in," Stephanie said.

"Leave him out there. He's an outdoor cat, Nick said."

"Speaking of Nick, have you heard from them yet?"

"No. I don't expect to until after they've checked out that church. It should be anytime, now."

CHAPTER SIXTY-FOUR

Selena fired at movement in the churchyard and heard a cry. "Three out here," she yelled. She saw a man run toward a large mausoleum. She fired again, two rounds. The dark shape fell to the ground. "Make it two."

Nick crawled over to her. Ronnie was shooting into the interior of the church. The shots echoed in the stone space. Bullets fired from the graveyard ricocheted around the stone vestibule and sent fragments flying through the air. The shooters couldn't get a clear shot, but they were doing a good job of keeping everyone occupied.

"You cover me while I run for that big tombstone over there." Nick pointed at a large, weeping angel, gray in the cold light. "Ready?"

Selena inserted a fresh magazine, nodded. She began squeezing off rapid shots. Nick got to his feet and ran flat out for the angel. Bullets kicked up dirt around his feet and caromed from the memorial, whining away into the night. One struck the heel of his boot and sent him sprawling. He rolled behind the monument and squatted down. His foot was numb. The heel of the boot was gone.

Lights were coming on in the rectory. Someone would be calling the cops. They didn't have much time. He darted a glance around the base of the angel, saw movement, fired. The figure collapsed. He saw no one else. There was a pause in the firing while Selena reloaded. Ronnie had stopped shooting. Was he hit? Nick put the thought aside.

He heard a vehicle start up. A dark van shot out from the other side of the church, past the main entrance and onto the road leading to town. Nick stood and fired after it until the slide locked back on his gun. It disappeared into the night. He reloaded and ran limping toward the church.

Selena got to her feet. Ronnie came out of the vestibule. "They kept me pinned down," he said. "They left and took the altar with them."

The rectory was ablaze with light. Nick thought he saw a curtain move at a window.

"Time to boogie," he said.

CHAPTER SIXTY-FIVE

"There wasn't anything else we could do," Nick said. "Whoever planned it knew we were coming. They set up an ambush and kept us busy while they grabbed the Ark."

"Are you sure it was the Ark?" Elizabeth asked.

Nick, Selena, Stephanie and Ronnie were gathered in Elizabeth's office. Burps slept on his back on a cat bed in the corner of the room. He snored. Elizabeth had bought the bed on a spur of the moment impulse. Now she was wondering why she had.

"I don't know, Director. But they took the whole altar with them. That makes me think the Ark was inside it."

"The altar was big enough," Selena said. "It was made from plain wood without decoration, like a big rectangular box. A Puritan would like an altar like that. It would never have occurred to anyone to see if there was something inside it."

"MI5 took over from the local bobbies," Elizabeth said, "to clean up after you. Automatic weapons aren't that usual in England. They were looking for terrorist connections."

"They find any?" Ronnie said.

"No. But all of the dead men were in the system. All former military. Two from SAS, one from our own Rangers. They found blood trails, so you probably winged a few more."

"Mercenaries," Nick said.

"MI5 identified one of them as having worked for a contractor security company called MKTA. It's run by a former SAS Colonel named McKenzie. MKTA has been implicated in a massacre at a refugee camp in Africa. They're suspect in other incidents as well."

"No proof it was them?"

"Nothing that would hold up in court."

"What's McKenzie's story? You don't make that kind of rank in SAS without serious skills. Why didn't he stay in?"

"He was forced to resign after he allowed the torture of Iraqi prisoners. He should have gone to prison."

"Someone must have hired him," Ronnie said.

"That's where it gets interesting," Stephanie said. "I found this."

The monitor on the wall came to life with a picture taken at Logan Airport in Boston. An unsmiling, hard looking man with a short haircut and sunglasses was passing through customs.

"That's McKenzie. He showed up right after you came back from your visit to Pembroke Castle."

She pressed a key. The next shot was taken outside the terminal. McKenzie was getting into a private limousine. The rear plate was easy to read in the photo.

"That's not an airport limo. It belongs to Phillip Harrison, the main player in Cask and Swords."

"The group Adam told me about."

"Harrison has a place up in Maine on a private island, but McKenzie flew back to London that same evening. So he must have met with Harrison in Boston."

"It backs up what Adam told me. Explains why a sociopath like McKenzie is hanging out with a big banker," Nick said.

"They kind of go together, don't they?" Ronnie said. "Sociopaths and big bankers?"

"Try to be serious, please." Harker picked up her pen. "Let's make some assumptions."

"Why would McKenzie's people be in that church?" Selena asked.

"Same reason as us," Nick said. "They were after the Ark. That's assumption number one."

Stephanie said, "Maybe they were after you."

"Why wait until we went to the church? How did they even know we'd be there? It makes more sense the other way."

"You have a point."

"If they were after the Ark and Harrison met with McKenzie, assumption number two is pretty obvious."

"Harrison hired McKenzie to find the Ark," Ronnie said.

"Right."

"So what's the next assumption?"

"How did they find the Ark?"

"The same way we did?" Selena asked.

"They didn't have the sword, or know about Cromwell. There's an easier way. Let us do it for them."

"They were following you," Elizabeth said, "and that's how they knew where to look. If they found a way to bug your conversations, that would tell them where."

"Pretty sophisticated, but it makes sense. McKenzie would know about that kind of technology."

"What's our next assumption?" Ronnie asked.

"That the Ark was hidden in the altar and McKenzie will bring it to Harrison. He may already have done it." Elizabeth set her pen down.

"We might still have a chance to intercept before he delivers it."

"We don't know where he'd hand it over to Harrison."

"I don't think he'd fly it into Boston," Selena said. "Or any other place where customs might want to take a look. He needs privacy, someplace remote."

"McKenzie owns a sea going yacht called the *Bristol Angel*," Stephanie said, "and Harrison owns that island in Maine."

She tapped a few keys. An aerial shot of the island came up on the wall monitor.

"This is it. It's pretty remote, up near Canada. McKenzie could take the Ark there. The weather is good. He could sail that boat across the Atlantic and never get near a customs port."

"Can we get a real time view of the island?" Nick asked.

"The satellite comes into range in about an hour. I can get something then."

"Let me guess," Ronnie said. "The next assumption is that if the Ark is on that island, someone has to go get it. Like us."

"Why we pay you big bucks, Ronnie."

"What's the name of this place?"

"Indian Island," Elizabeth said. "You ought to feel right at home."

CHAPTER SIXTY-SIX

Nick, Ronnie and Selena studied satellite photos of Harrison's island.

"About a mile long," Ronnie said, "maybe half a mile wide."

"Mostly rocks and trees," Nick said.

"It looks like the dock below the house is the only decent landing spot."

"There has to be another place we can land." Nick tugged on his ear.

"I went over the charts with Lamont," Ronnie said. "The water around the island is full of rocks and currents. It's unpredictable. Treacherous on a good day."

"This is where we could use Lamont," Nick said. "Guess you can't have everything."

"He spotted a place on the north shore where we could get a raft in, here." Ronnie marked one of the photos. "We'll have to use a Zodiac. It'll be tricky, but I don't see any way to take in a boat."

"Raft it is."

"What about security?" Selena asked. "Harrison is bound to have cameras. Maybe dogs, sensors."

"I don't see any kennels," Nick said, "but he must have people walking around. We'll have to play it by ear. Once we're on shore, there's good cover. It's thick woods. I think we can get close without much trouble. The house is a different story. It's clear all around, no cover at all."

"What's this building here?" Selena asked. She indicated a rectangular structure about a hundred feet from the house. A graveled drive led from there to the house.

"Looks like an equipment shed of some kind, or a big garage."

"The trees come right up to it. We could make that the first objective."

Nick nodded. "That would work. We go at night. We make it to that building, get out of sight and make sure everyone's asleep. Then we move on the house."

Stephanie came into the room. "New pics from our eye in the sky," she said. "You want to see these."

She put one of the pictures on the table. "Harrison showed up late yesterday. That's him."

The picture had been taken from 80,000 feet but looked as though it had been shot by someone close by. Harrison was wearing a short sleeved shirt, light pants and boat shoes. He had his hands in his pockets. His face was easily recognizable.

"The satellite made another pass this morning, around two hours ago." She spread several pictures on the table. A sleek vessel had tied up at the end of the pier. They could make out the name on the stern of the boat. It was the *Bristol Angel*, McKenzie's yacht. A man stood on the dock, hands on his hips.

"That's Nigel McKenzie."

Four men were lifting a wooden crate from somewhere below decks. In the next picture, Phillip Harrison could be seen walking toward McKenzie. As the progression of pictures continued, Harrison and McKenzie shook hands and stood watching while the crate was moved to the pier.

"That's it. The satellite went out of range."

"Thanks, Steph."

"Let me know if you need anything else." She went back upstairs.

"Question is, did they take that box to the house or one of the other buildings?" Ronnie said.

"And is it the Ark?" Selena said.

"Pack your bathing suit," Nick said.

CHAPTER SIXTY-SEVEN

The moon was an electric, cold light glittering off the white froth of the Atlantic. The raft rose and fell and slapped hard against the uneven chop, sending showers of salt spray over them. A stiff breeze brought the smell of pine and earth. They were close to the island.

They wore black combat gear with full body armor. Each had a SIG-Sauer P229 and an MP-5N slung across the chest. Reliable, accurate and deadly, with a high rate of fire. It would work if it was drenched in water.

Selena and Nick rode in the center of a Navy Seal CRRC, a Zodiac. The inflatable raft had separate, water-tight compartments that might keep it from sinking if there was a puncture or tear. A fuel cell in the front fed the engine with a rubber hose. Ronnie was at the tiller, navigating with his GPS. The outboard engine was a two stroke impeller type with pump-jet propulsion, rated at 55 horses. It was quiet for an outboard but it wasn't completely silent. Nick wasn't much worried about the noise. It was a reasonable bet that guards wouldn't patrol this far away from the house. This end of the island was covered with a thick stand of trees. The swirling ocean currents and heavy surf were an effective deterrent. He watched the shore draw closer and understood why.

Sharp rocks rose black and wet and ragged in the moonlight. They stuck out of the dark waters like the teeth of a giant sea-beast lying in wait for its prey. The Atlantic whirled and churned about them, turning the surface into a frenzy of foam. The waves made a deep, booming noise as they dashed themselves to spray on the rocks, drowning out the sound of the motor.

"There's the gap," Ronnie said. He pointed at a narrow channel filled with white foam between two tall rocks. "Once we're through, it will be calm. The shore's about fifty yards past."

He opened the throttle. The raft surged forward, slapping the waves.

Selena held on tight where she sat. *I don't like this,* she thought. *I don't like this at all.* She watched the rocks getting closer. The nearer they got, the sharper they looked. They entered the gap.

The water gripped the raft in a relentless fist. The raft swerved right and turned sideways.

"Current!" Ronnie yelled.

They struck the rocks. Selena heard the fabric rip open against the hard, sharp surface. The fuel cell ruptured. A pungent mix of gas and oil sprayed over her boots. Air rushed out of the front of the raft and water poured over the edge. The raft dipped and tilted and slammed against the rocks and she was thrown into the icy water. The Zodiac swung back and hit her in the head.

She went under, the weight of her gear pulling her down. A sudden, sharp pain cut through her pants and into her leg. The salt water was like fire in the wound. She fought the current, desperate for air, and broke the surface. She had time to draw in a breath before she was sucked under again. She fought the undertow and struggled and kicked until she broke into the air again.

The current let her go. She looked around for the others.

The raft was a crumpled mass, hung fast on the unforgiving rocks. The shredded fabric tossed and bobbed in the waves. She saw Ronnie break the surface not far away, then Nick.

They swam toward the shore until they could set their feet down and wade onto the island. The beach was a strip of fist-sized rocks and strewn sea wrack, six or seven feet wide. She fell to her knees, exhausted.

"Keep moving. Into the woods," Nick said. They got inside the line of trees and Nick held up his hand.

"All right. We deal with it." He saw the gash on Selena's leg. "You're hurt."

She looked down. Blood welled from the cut, black under the moon. She took her knife and slit the pants leg so she could see the wound. It was a nasty, ragged gash almost a foot long.

"Help me get it bandaged," she said.

Each of them carried a compact med kit designed for a quick patch in the field. Basic stuff to stop bleeding, stave off infection, sew something up, or bandage it. Nick began working on her.

"Going to leave a scar," he said. "You have to stop this. You'll catch up to me."

"Maybe I'll get a tattoo over it after it heals." She winced as Nick bandaged the injury. "Hearts and flowers in a vine. Or guns and roses."

"Death before dishonor," Ronnie said.

"A big heart with Mom inside it," Nick said. He stood. "Try it out."

She stood. It hurt, but the leg felt solid under her.

"Just a scratch," she said. "I'm fine."

"Okay. We lost the comm gear, the night vision stuff and the extra ammo, but we still have our weapons. Check to see what you've got for ammo."

They checked the pockets of their uniforms.

"Three extra mags for the MP-5, one in the gun," Ronnie said. "Two mags for the pistol, plus one in."

"My spare MP-5 mags are gone," Selena said. "Just the one in. I've got two extras for the pistol, one in."

"And I'm the same as Ronnie. Here." Nick handed her one of his MP-5 backups. Ronnie did the same. She put them in a pocket and shivered.

"90 rounds each. Make 'em count," Nick said. "It's cold, but we'll warm up as we move through the woods. We can't risk a fire. Check your weapons, dry things out as best you can. They'll work if they're wet, but get the water out."

"Your phone work?" Ronnie asked.

Nick took out the pouch with his phone. The pouch was soaked. He took the phone out. There was no signal.

"Nada. Maybe later."

They worked on drying out the guns. Then they set off through the woods for the garage near Harrison's house.

Somewhere in the darkness an owl hooted, a long, mournful cry.

CHAPTER SIXTY-EIGHT

At 4:00 A.M. Elizabeth came into her office and found a dead mouse lying by her chair. Burps had been leaving little presents for her. This morning it was a mouse. Yesterday it had been a garter snake. She put the small corpse in her wastebasket.

That darn cat is courting me, she thought.

Stephanie came in with a cup of coffee. Steam wafted from the cup.

"Thanks, Steph."

Elizabeth took the cup and blew on the hot, black liquid. She wasn't surprised to find Steph here and working. Most days they were both in by 5:00 A.M. Today, Elizabeth had quit at midnight and slept in the living quarters downstairs. That had been happening a lot, lately. She'd taken to keeping changes of clothing and back up toiletries downstairs, just in case.

"Israel just shot down a drone Hezbollah sent from Lebanon," Stephanie said. "That's the second one this week."

"I don't know why they think those will work. Iran sends the parts to Lebanon, Hezbollah assembles them and sends them off, Israel shoots them down. What's the point?"

"Prestige booster for Hezbollah's leaders. Look at us, we are doing God's work against the Zionist enemy, all that BS. Hezbollah is a serious opponent, though. They fought Israel to a stalemate during the last invasion."

"That was political. I don't think they can stop the Israelis this time around," Elizabeth said. "Lerner is going to give it everything he's got. It's a matter of hours at most before he moves. That drone may be the last thing he needs to justify an invasion."

On Elizabeth's desk was a small device which had only one purpose. It displayed the current defense condition level in colored letters and numerals. When Rice had raised the level to DEFCON3, the color had changed from yellow-green to yellow. Now the device beeped three times. The display changed to orange. It said DEFCON2.

Elizabeth looked at it and felt as though she'd swallowed a lead ball. Her phone rang.

"Harker." She listened for a moment. "Steph, bring up the SBIRS system on the monitor. And whatever we've got over the Middle East."

SBIRS stood for Satellite Based Infrared Surveillance. Two dozen birds in geostationary and moving orbits formed a grid that covered the globe. It was one of the key strategic assets in America's intelligence network. SBIRS had been built primarily to monitor, track and help destroy a hostile missile launch.

"Thank you, Clarence." Elizabeth hung up the phone. She turned to Stephanie.

"That was DCI Hood. There's activity at Badr missile base in Iran. Hood was giving me a heads up. He's worried that the Israelis may have learned Iran has a nuke."

"Badr is where they have the Shahab 3-B," Stephanie said. "What if they put that nuke on one of those?"

Elizabeth gestured at the orange display with it's chilling message. "Rice has called a meeting of the National Security Council in case they did."

"If Tehran uses that Russian warhead, Israel will annihilate them," Stephanie said. "They have enough nukes to wipe Iran off the map."

"What worries me is that the Mullahs might be crazy enough to think they could win with a preemptive strike. The Shahab 3B has a very short launch time and sophisticated avoidance capabilities. Once it's up it would be hard to stop in time."

"Doesn't Israel have Patriot missile defenses?"

"Yes, and their own Arrow 2. But the 3B has a new evasion system. It could get through."

"The pictures are up," Stephanie said.

The monitor image was in real time, from a geo-stationary satellite over Iran. The Badr missile base was east of Tehran in the Central Semnan desert, a desolate, dry wasteland. They were looking at the reason Rice had gone to DEFCON2. Hundreds of heat signatures moved about the base. There was intense activity around the silos.

"They could be getting ready to launch," Stephanie said.

Elizabeth watched the images and the computer readouts on the right of the display.

"If they do," she said, "it's a new ball game."

CHAPTER SIXTY-NINE

Nick and the others lay just inside the edge of the trees, fifty feet away from Harrison's garage. The building had one window on the side. There was a side entry door. A John Deere riding mower was parked out front on the gravel. Nick watched a guard walking his route between the garage and the main house. He'd been watching the man for an hour. The guard had an M-16 slung on his shoulder.

"Same pattern, all the time," Nick said. "He goes past the house, around it, comes back and down the drive to the front of the garage, walks around the building, goes back to the house and does it all over again. It takes him about twenty minutes."

"He looks bored out of his skull," Ronnie said. "Reminds me of guarding barracks filled with snoring jarheads against enemy attacks from crazed Californians."

"Pendleton?"

"Yeah."

"You never know, Ronnie. Might have got invaded from Tijuana."

"Or San Diego."

"Next time he's behind the house, we go for that door."

"I've got my picks." Ronnie patted a pocket. "Looks simple from here."

Five minutes later, the guard disappeared behind the house. The three got up and ran for the garage. Selena felt the gash on her leg open under the bandage as she ran. Ronnie inserted the picks, jiggled the tumblers. The lock clicked. They pulled the door open and went inside. Selena closed it behind them.

The interior was dim with faint light coming from two skylights overhead and a small window on each side. Three shrouded vehicles were parked against the back wall. Ronnie lifted a corner on one and peered underneath.

"An old Bentley," he said. "Collector car."

A Ford pickup was parked near the closed doors in front. Tools hung over a long workbench. It was a typical, neat garage, except for boards and straw packing lying on the floor near a wooden crate by the doors. From where they stood they couldn't see what it contained.

"Think that's it?" Selena said.

"Only one way to find out." They moved forward until they could see the contents.

"It's the altar from the church," Ronnie said. "The front is loose."

He lifted the front of the altar away. The space inside was empty.

"Something was in there."

"They must have taken it into the house," Nick said.

"What now, Kemo Sabe?"

"We go get it. The house is dark. They're asleep. No point in waiting."

"We lost the trank guns," Selena said. "What about the guard?"

"We have to silence him. There's no way we get over there without him seeing us. We'll take him out when he makes a pass behind the garage."

"He should be due any time now," Ronnie said.

"We'll see him go by the window. I'll take him down."

They moved to the door.

They waited in silence. A few moments later the guard passed by the window, headed for the back of the building. Nick gave it a beat, then eased out of the door. The night air was thick with the sound of crickets. The man was just disappearing around the corner.

Nick came up behind him, silent as the mist rising from the ground. The guard sensed something and began to turn, too late. Nick wrapped his arm around in a choke hold. The guard struggled and twisted, making choking sounds as he tried to call out. Nick kept pressure on the carotid arteries. The man stopped moving and slumped, unconscious. Nick dragged him back to the door and into the garage.

Ronnie found electrical wire on the workbench. They hogtied the guard and stuffed an oily rag into his mouth.

They stepped out into the moonlight. The crickets had gone silent.

"The camera on the porch is pointed at the entrance," Nick said. "If we keep to the side of the house, we should be all right."

One of the windows on the side of the house showed a sliver of dim light.

"They're still awake in there. Keep your weapons ready."

"I thought you wanted to wait until they were asleep," Selena said.

"Too late for that. The guard had a radio. He probably reports in on a regular schedule. We have to move now."

"Are we supposed to shoot anyone we see?"

"They didn't mind shooting at us in England."

"We don't know if it's the same people. Maybe Harrison just hired those men."

"It doesn't matter. He's behind it. Don't shoot unless you have to, but don't hesitate if you do."

Selena let it go.

"There has to be a back entrance. Keep together. Go."

They ran across the lawn, away from the camera, to the side of the house.

They bent low under the windows and moved to the back. A wide screened porch ran the length of the house. There was a camera on the corner, pointed toward a short flight of steps. Ronnie took a spray can from his pack, reached up and covered the lens. They went up the steps, opened a screen door and moved to the back entrance, a door with a brass knob. Nick tried the knob. It was unlocked. Harrison wasn't expecting trouble. Nick held up three fingers and counted down. On the third count he opened the door. It led into a large laundry area.

They were in the house.

On the far side of the laundry room was a closed wooden door painted white. Nick cracked it and listened. Then he eased the door open the rest of the way.

A long, carpeted hall led away into the house. Flickering light spilled out from a room on the side. They moved silently down the hall. When Nick reached the open doorway he held up his hand and listened. Inside the room, someone was humming to himself.

Nick knelt down and risked a quick glance around the door frame. The room was a study. Books lined one wall. The windows were covered by cloth drapes. A man sat in a chair, his back to the door. The humming noise was coming from him. The tune was vaguely familiar. It might have been a hymn.

In front of the seated figure was a large, mahogany table, polished to a dark gleam. The light in the room came from a dozen fat candles that filled the room with a deep, rich glow. The light reflected off gold. Resplendent in the middle of the table was the Ark of the Covenant.

CHAPTER SEVENTY

The Ark was a little less than four feet long and covered in thin sheets of hammered gold. It was two feet wide and two high, small enough to fit inside the altar stolen from St. John's. The gold had fallen away in spots, exposing dark wood underneath. *Cedar, maybe,* Nick thought.

Regular, geometric designs were stamped into the gold. Two golden figures knelt on the lid with heads bowed, their long wings extended toward the middle of the Ark.

The cherubim. Just like in the Bible.

An elaborate, carved railing went around the lid. There were supposed to be rings for poles to carry the Ark, but they were missing. One of the feet was gone. The others were carved like lion's claws.

They moved into the room. The man in the chair stopped humming. He still had his back to them.

"McKenzie?" he said. "I thought you went to bed." He rose and turned toward the door.

It was Phillip Harrison. His face went white when he saw the guns pointing at him.

"Who...? What are you doing here?"

"Ronnie, watch the hall," Nick said. Ronnie took up station by the door. His MP-5 was a dull black in the candlelight.

"Do you know who I am?" Harrison said.

"Why do big shots always say that when they get caught?" Nick asked. "Like it should make a difference. I know who you are, Harrison. You're someone who's about to spend a long time in a very unpleasant place."

"How dare you."

"That's the other thing they always say," said Selena.

"I don't know who you are, but you have made a very serious mistake." Harrison had regained his composure.

Over his shoulder, Ronnie said, "Can this guy say anything original?"

Selena was looking at the Ark. "It's beautiful," she said.

"Do you know what this is?" Harrison looked at Nick. His eyes had an odd gleam in the flickering light.

He's nuts, Nick thought. *Something about the eyes.*

"I have been searching for this for years. God spoke to me. He brought this to me. Do you really think He will let you take it away?"

"God talks to you?" Nick said. His ear itched. He reached up to scratch it.

"Nick." It was Ronnie. "Someone coming."

"Selena, cover him. Harrison, you try anything, she'll shoot you. Do you understand?"

"I don't believe you."

"You should," Selena said. "You killed my friend. Sit down." She poked him in the chest with the barrel of her MP-5 and gestured at the chair. It was a persuasive argument. Harrison saw the expression on her face and sat down.

To the right of the door the hall ran along the side of the house and ended at a tee on the far end. The other way led back to the laundry room and the porch. Ronnie saw a quick movement at the tee end. Someone ducked back out of sight.

"Company," he said. "They must have found the guard."

"How many?"

"I don't know. What do you want to do?"

Nick's ear was burning. He tugged on it. A round object rolled down the hall and stopped short of the door.

"Grenade," Ronnie yelled. He ducked back into the room.

The grenade was a flash bang. It went off in the hall with a deafening blast and blinding white light. The warning and being inside the room kept him from being blinded, but the noise and the concussion gave Nick an instant headache. He was dizzy. He reached blindly around the door frame and fired at the end of the hall.

Selena was stunned by the sound. Harrison jumped up and wrapped his arms around her and reached for the gun. She struggled against his bear hug and they staggered into the table. It tipped. Candles fell over and rolled across the floor. One came to rest under the cloth drape, still burning. The ark tilted and crashed onto the floor. One of the cherubim broke into pieces.

Nick and Ronnie fired into the hall. Answering shots came from both ends.

The drapes in the study were old, sewn in a day long before the thought of fireproof chemicals. Shimmering blue fire shot straight up the cloth. Suddenly the window was engulfed in a sheet of flame. The house had wooden floors and ceilings built of dry Maine pine. Flames crawled along the ceiling and found the paper books and wooden shelves. The wall caught fire. The room filled with heat and thick, black smoke. Smoke roiled out of the open door, into the hall.

Selena head butted Harrison in the face. He loosened his grip. She kneed him in the groin. She got her left arm free and brought her fist around and punched him hard in the ear. He yelled. She broke his grip and brought the MP-5 across and slammed it into his head. He went down on the floor, unconscious. On an impulse, she reached down beside him and grabbed a golden piece of the broken cherubim with her left hand.

"Selena!" Nick yelled.

She ran to the door, coughing, clutching the piece of ancient wood, her MP-5 in her right hand. She smelled her hair curling from the heat. She looked back. The Ark was burning with golden light.

"Harrison," she said. She started back into the room. Part of the ceiling came down in a cascade of sparks and flame. Nick grabbed her arm.

"Leave him. Go left. Lay down fire as we go."

They went out the door, guns blazing. The hall was choked with smoke. Bullets came from beyond the smoke, smacking into the walls. They ran. A round smashed into Nick's armor and knocked him down. Ronnie pulled him to his feet.

Nick felt sharp pain with every breath as he ran. *Cracked a rib,* he thought, *for sure.*

They reached the back porch. Behind them, the hall filled with dense smoke. Flickering, orange-red light glowed in the choking clouds. Shots from outside ripped through the porch screens as they burst through the back door. Glass shattered behind them. Ronnie and Nick fired at the same time and a voice cried out. Selena triggered a burst and her gun locked open. She couldn't hold onto the piece of the Ark and load a magazine at the same time. She let the MP-5 hang from its sling and drew her pistol and began firing at moving shadows as they ran for the woods.

Then they were in the safety of the trees.

Behind them, the house burned with fierce, roaring flames. The fire broke through the roof. Glass blew out of the windows as the flames raced through the upper stories. Nick had never seen anything burn so fast.

No one was shooting at them anymore. They moved farther back into the trees.

Then the house exploded. The burning roof lifted into the air. A column of flame a hundred feet high erupted into the night.

"Holy shit," Ronnie said.

They ducked as debris whistled through the woods and burning pieces rained down from the sky.

"Must have had something nasty in the basement," Nick said.

They waited. No one came after them. The sound of big diesel engines starting up came from the direction of the water.

"McKenzie's boat," Nick said. "He's leaving."

Ronnie looked a question.

"No, let him go," Nick said. "We'll let someone else worry about it."

He coughed and gasped and bent over in pain.

"You're hurt," Selena said.

"Armor saved me. But I think I've got a couple of broken ribs."

He looked at her. Her face was blackened, one side of her hair was singed.

"Let's find a boat and get out of here," Ronnie said.

Nick looked at the fire raging where the house had been. "The Ark is gone."

"Not all of it." Selena held up the piece of the broken cherubim.

CHAPTER SEVENTY-ONE

The piece of the Ark lay on Elizabeth's desk. It was the kneeling figure of a cherubim, minus the wings. They had broken off when the lid struck the floor.

The figure was carved from a solid piece of wood, finished with a flat base. Some of the thin gold covering remained, some had been lost in the mad dash from the burning house. Now was the first time they'd all had a chance to examine it.

But it wasn't the first time Selena had looked at it. She hadn't even told Nick what she'd found.

"It's hard to believe you found the Ark and now it's gone," Stephanie said. "It's a terrible loss."

"Maybe it's not quite what you think," Selena said.

"What do you mean?"

"Director, take a look at the bottom of the cherubim, on the lower right corner. You have to look close."

Harker picked up the fragment and turned it over. She peered at the lower corner.

"I don't see...wait a minute." She got a magnifying glass out of a drawer and held it over the piece.

"This can't be right. There's something written here." She read it out loud.

Bernardus fecit me anno domini MCCCVII.

"That's Latin. What's Latin doing there?"

"Exactly," Selena said. "It says *'Bernard made me in the Year of Our Lord 1307'.*"

The silence was electric. Nick found his voice.

"You mean the Ark was a fake?"

"Yes. That inscription was under the cherubim, where no one would ever see it. The ark we saw was made in 1307, by someone named Bernard. Probably a Templar."

"Why make a fake?" Ronnie said.

"Deception," Selena said. "1307 was a bad year for the Templars. De Molay suspected treachery. I think they had the real Ark and he ordered a copy made in case King Phillip and the Pope managed to seize the Templar treasure. The letter was probably meant to throw them off the scent."

"But they never found it."

"No."

"Then it may still exist," Harker said.

"Along with the rest of the Templar treasure."

Nick started laughing.

"Want to share the joke, Nick?"

"Sorry, Director. All those clues we followed. For a fake. Harrison went to a lot of trouble chasing it down and got himself killed. All for a fake."

The alarm on Elizabeth's desk beeped five times. The display turned red.

DEFCON1.

Elizabeth's phone rang. She picked up, listened, set it back down.

"Stephanie, pull up the Iranian missile base."

Stephanie's fingers flashed over her keyboard. The monitor lit with a live shot of the missile base at Badr. There was frenzied activity on the ground.

"The silos are hot," Nick said. "Look at those heat signatures."

"They're going to launch." Elizabeth was pale. "If they've mounted that nuke, all hell is going to break loose. Steph, give me a split screen over Israel. Rabat-David Air base, in the north."

A second picture appeared on the screen. Rabat-David was one of Israel's major air bases, home to a large part of the

Israeli Air Force. Planes were taking off at a steady rate. Nick saw dozens more waiting.

"They're putting everything into the air," Nick said.

"Switch to Egozi," Harker said.

Egozi military base wasn't on the tourist maps of Israel. It was where the Israelis kept their nuclear missiles in underground silos.

"The silos are opening up," Ronnie said.

They were. The silo openings had been camouflaged under desert sands. Now they were opening to the air. White vapor rose from the openings. Israel was preparing to launch.

"They're launching in Iran," Stephanie said. Her voice was hoarse.

The screen showed intense heat at one of the silos, then at half a dozen more. The missiles began to rise into the air. At lift off, the deadly shapes were still visible. It was like watching a slow motion ballet of death.

"Oh, Jesus," Ronnie said.

Then the screen went white in a violent burst of light and blanked out.

"What happened?"

"I don't know." They watched. The image returned, distorted with lines of static and visual debris. A towering mushroom cloud rose into the desert sky over Iran. The missile base at Badr had disappeared. There was no sign of any of the Iranian missiles, no readouts of projected trajectories, arrival times, targets. They were all gone.

No one said anything. They watched the cloud, billowing up into the atmosphere.

Elizabeth's phone rang.

CHAPTER SEVENTY-TWO

President James Rice sat in a comfortable, brown leather chair at the head of a long table in the Situation Room, watching events spin out of control.

This can't be happening, he thought. But it was, right in front of him.

Air Force officers and technicians manned a long console and monitored satellite feeds to a dozen screens set on the wall. Others present in the room included General Price from the Joint Chiefs, the National Security Advisor, Hood from CIA and the Secretary of Defense. The Vice-President was on his way to shelter in West Virginia, just in case. The Secretary of State was in England. Marine One idled on the White House lawn, ready to ferry Rice to Andrews and Air Force One in case he decided to take his command center airborne.

The Israeli and Iranian force deployments were laid out on the screens for all to see. The Middle East crawled with military activity. Israel's planes were in the air and heading for Iran. The Iranian silos were hot. The Israeli silos were going hot. Iran was scrambling its fighters.

The Israeli PM and the Iranian Supreme Leader were not responding to calls from the White House. Half a dozen world leaders were clamoring for the President's attention. The only ones Rice was talking to were the Russians and the Chinese, the only ones that mattered at the moment. He had them on speakers so the others could hear.

"Mister President, this is a very dangerous situation."

It was the Russian, Gorovsky. Someone spoke in simultaneous translation on his end as he spoke. Rice considered him a brutish man. Brutish, but smart. It wouldn't do to underestimate him.

"It has been made more so by Iran's acquisition of one of your warheads," Rice said.

He didn't want to get into a pissing match with the Russians, but the only thing they respected was force and the willingness to confront.

"We provided no such armaments. But you have armed the Jews."

"Not with nukes," Rice said. "The Israelis did that for themselves."

"With your help. Mister President, our satellites show that you have gone to your highest state of alert."

"As have you, President Gorovsky."

"We would be foolish not to."

"If you see that, you know that we have not released our bombers. They are at the fail safe points, as are all our forces. As, I might add, are yours."

"We do not wish for war." There was just a note of conciliation in the Russian's voice.

"Mister President." It was the Chinese leader's voice.

An Air Force Colonel watching the console said, "Sir, there's been a nuclear explosion in Iran."

Russia and China were tracking events with their own satellites. Excited voices crackled from the speakers. Rice watched the distinctive cloud boiling up into the Iranian sky. His stomach clenched.

"Whose was it?" he said.

"We don't know, yet. We have to wait for analysis."

"How big?"

"Hard to say, sir. Maybe a megaton. Possibly less. Not more."

"A missile warhead?"

"Yes, sir. There were no planes in the area. We picked up nothing coming in. They launched, then the nuke went off."

"We need to know where that nuke came from. How soon can we find out?"

"Working on it, sir."

"President Gorovsky. Premier Li," Rice said. "Please, let us not do anything in haste."

"The Israelis have attacked Iran with nuclear weapons," Gorovsky said. His voice was angry, agitated. "This cannot be tolerated."

"We don't know that," Rice said. "Perhaps not. We detected no incoming missiles or planes. It may be an accident. A systems failure on an Iranian missile."

"A nuclear accident in Iran? On one of their missile bases?" It was Premier Li. "Iran does not have nuclear capability. We are certain of this."

"Not yet, they don't," Rice said. "But our intelligence says they have a warhead. An old SS-13, from the days of the Soviet Union."

"Ah," Li said.

Gorovsky blustered. "We had nothing to do with this. The Russian Federation wants only peace. We are signatories on the non-proliferation treaties. We do not sell nuclear weapons to others. If a warhead was obtained by Iran, it was not Russian."

"Of course, Mister President." Rice was soothing. "We are well aware of your efforts to limit the spread of such weapons. No one suggests you are responsible in any way."

The Chairman of the Joint Chiefs rolled his eyes. Everyone in the room knew that an unknown number of Russian nukes had been stolen or gone missing when the Soviet Union collapsed. The latest intelligence estimates set the number at no less than 80.

An officer entered the room and held a whispered conversation with the Chairman of the Joint Chiefs.

"Mister President."

"Yes, General?"

"We had a low orbit bird in the area and managed to get readings from the cloud. The radiation signature is unique. The bomb was Russian, manufactured at Mayak. It wasn't Israeli."

Every nuclear bomb or warhead manufactured anywhere in the world contained uranium or plutonium with distinctive markers that allowed accurate identification of its origin. Mayak had been Russia's major facility for nuclear weapons production for many years.

"You're certain?"

"Yes, sir."

"You heard that, President Gorovsky?" Rice said.

"We did not attack Iran!"

"No, of course not. Iran acquired a missile illegally and it failed when they tried to launch. They destroyed their own base. No one is blaming you, Mister President."

He turned to General Price.

"General, have the Israelis launched?"

"No, sir. They can see the same thing we do."

Rice decided to gamble. It was a big gamble, if he was wrong. But the news that this wasn't an Israeli strike altered things.

"President Gorovsky, Chairman Li, I believe we must halt this before it goes any farther. I am ordering our forces to stand down one level. General Price, please go to DEFCON2."

"Sir..."

"DEFCON2, General."

Price was reluctant. "Yes, sir." He took out his phone, spoke into it. "Confirmed, sir."

"Thank you, General."

Gorovsky's voice was tense, but something had changed. "I will also stand back," he said. They heard him giving the orders.

"We shall do the same." It was Li.

"Gentlemen," Rice said. "Perhaps this time we can forge a new beginning. Let us use this terrible incident to find new ways to rein in these weapons. Now I am going to call the Prime Minister in Israel."

"I will see what I can do with Tehran," Gorovsky said.

"Perhaps a summit in Beijing might be a good idea," Li said. "Neutral ground for Tehran and Jerusalem."

"An excellent idea," Rice said. "Thank you, gentlemen." He ended the call and turned to Price.

"Keep an eye on those bastards," he said. "I don't trust either one of them. Keep our subs at DEFCON1."

Price looked relieved. "Yes, Mister President."

CHAPTER SEVENTY-THREE

"It was a rough week," Nick said.

He was sitting in the shrink's office. Milton nodded politely.

"I can't tell you exactly what I did."

Milton waited.

"I was thinking about the last time I was here. You remember what we were talking about?"

"You said you felt helpless. About the grenade."

"Yeah. Well, more than that. It's not just that grenade. What I do...it could happen again."

"I know."

"You do?"

"You carry a gun. You're no longer in the military. I would guess you face situations like that grenade more often than you'd like."

"You saw in the papers, about Israel and Iran?"

"Pretty hard to miss."

"Something else I can't control. Wars other people start."

"How do you feel about it? That incident?"

"They teach you that phrase in shrink school? How do you feel?"

Milton smiled. "First thing. Well, almost. So, how do you feel?"

"The same as with the grenade. Only more general. There's nothing I can do about it if the idiots running the world start throwing nukes at each other."

"Idiots is a harsh word."

"I don't think so. If anything, it's too mild."

Milton was quiet. Then, "How are you doing with the dreams?"

"I've been too tired to dream."

It wasn't true.

"You do anything to relax?"

"Have a drink. Read a book, sometimes."

"You looked pretty stiff when you walked in here."

Stiff was an understatement. He had two broken ribs from the round he'd taken in Maine. His back was tight. His neck was sore.

"It's nothing."

Milton looked at him, waited.

"I'm still having the dream."

Milton nodded.

"It's screwing up my love life."

"Is that all?"

"All what?"

"All that's screwed up?"

"Maybe it's more than just the dream doing it. All I know is I'm tired. I feel like I can't connect with Selena, not like we used to anyway."

"Go back to helpless."

"What do you mean?"

"Remember, you said you felt helpless when the grenade was coming at you."

"So?"

"Helpless about what?"

Nick could feel himself tensing up. "You know what. The grenade."

"The grenade is just a grenade."

...the grenade is coming toward him, turning end over end, a lopsided throw. It will kill him...he starts to move but it's too late...

He became very still. A shudder of energy passed through him. He'd always thought the dream was about guilt over killing the child. In that moment of stillness he saw that it wasn't about that. Not at all. The grenade had made him know he wasn't invincible. That he was no different from anyone else. That he could die a violent, painful death, just like all the others he'd seen die over the years. He'd never admitted it to himself, even after years of war. Never seen the simple truth of it. Suddenly it seemed obvious.

He looked at Milton.

"I could have died."

Milton waited.

"I never let myself ...I wouldn't let myself feel it."

Milton nodded. "It's alright," he said. "You don't have to be Captain America all the time."

It felt as if a great weight he hadn't known he carried had suddenly been taken from him.

CHAPTER SEVENTY-FOUR

Nick left his building for his evening run and saw Adam's armored Cadillac waiting for him. *Here we go again,* he thought. He got into the car. The door closed. They pulled away.

The car was still the same inside. Black leather, new and comfortable. Blacked out windows that let nothing through. Black partitions behind the driver and along the middle of the rear compartment. Speaker grill next to his ear.

"Hello, Nick."

The distorted electronic voice was the same. Nothing ever seemed to change inside this car except his future.

"Adam."

"I hope you hadn't planned anything for this evening."

This was new. "Nothing special."

"Good. Please give me your cell phone and your gun." A drawer slid open in the partition. "You can have them back later."

Something else that was new. Adam had never made the request before. Nick had a small Colt .380 he took on his runs. With hollow points, it had enough hydrostatic shock potential to stop almost anyone.

He stalled. "Why do you want them?"

"It's a condition. I'm sorry, but it's necessary. As I said, you will get them back."

The gun and phone were useless inside the car anyway. Nick put them in the tray. It slid shut.

"Where are we going?"

"You'll see. Good work with the ark."

That Adam knew what had happened didn't surprise Nick at all. He always seemed to know what Nick had been doing.

"McKenzie got away," Nick said.

"We know where he is. It's not important at the moment."

We.

"Director Harker thinks others were involved with Harrison," Nick said. "In his secret society."

"They were. That also doesn't matter at the moment."

Nick wondered what did matter. He was out of small talk. The speaker was silent.

He guessed they'd been riding for about a half hour when the car came to a smooth halt. There was a pause, then the car moved forward again and stopped. Nick waited for the door to unlock. He heard the click. He got out and stood by the car.

He was inside a large hanger or warehouse. It was mostly dark. The floor was cement. The car was parked under a bright light. The air was cool. The building smelled faintly of dust and construction.

Ahead of him was a dimly lit gallery set off by a partition of glass. He could make out the seated silhouettes of seven people behind the glass. One of them was a woman. It was impossible to make out the features of the people sitting there. A speaker grill was set in the wall under the partition. Adam's voice came through the grill.

"I apologize for the dramatics, Nick, but it's better this way. You cannot identify us. It has been decided you should know more about who we are."

"And you're going to tell me?" All his senses were on full alert. His ear was quiet.

Adam chuckled. "In a general sense. We are the Guardians."

You have got to be kidding, Nick thought. *Guardians of what?*

Adam continued. "Our organization goes back to the time of the Templars. I am our spokesman."

"You're Templars?"

"There have always been Templars dedicated to our task. When the Order was forced to go underground, our group was formed."

Nick was at a loss for words. Finally, he said, "For what purpose?"

"To guard the Ark. To preserve what is good in the world against the forces that would overwhelm it."

"That's a tall order," Nick said. "Why are you telling me this? What's the point of this meeting?"

He was getting angry. He wasn't sure why. Maybe because of the cloak and dagger set up. Or maybe he was tired of being manipulated by forces he couldn't control. He thought of the shrink, Milton. He'd probably approve of that thought.

"AEON is the point of this meeting," Adam said.

Nick knew about AEON. It was a centuries-old conspiracy that spanned the globe, an organization dedicated to dominating the world. Because of AEON, Selena had almost been killed. Because of AEON, the world had almost tipped into nuclear war.

Adam's voice sounded deep and metallic through the speaker. "We are the counterbalance to AEON. You and your group have been effective in helping us block them. We want you to inform Director Harker of our existence and establish a communication protocol. It is a precaution, in case a time should arise when it is not possible to meet with you as I have done in the past."

Meaning if I get killed, Nick thought, *or he does. There has to be a reason for the armored car.* Adam had established trust with Nick. Now he wanted Nick to set up contact with Harker, something that would never happen without that trust.

"Why reveal yourselves to me now? What's changed?"

"The world is approaching a turning point," Adam said. "AEON must not succeed in their plans for control and domination. The events in Russia were a disaster for them. It set off an internal struggle for control of the organization. That has now been resolved and they are renewing their agenda. There is a certain amount of danger involved for me. We felt that revealing our existence at this point would give more weight to our request and prepare you if a new connection must be made."

That didn't sound good. From what he'd seen, Nick thought Adam was well protected. If he was worried, something bad was in the wind.

Nick needed time to think. He changed the subject. "The Ark Harrison had in Maine was a forgery, a replica. Did you know that?"

"Yes. We have the genuine one. We have kept it safe since the Order found it concealed on the Temple Mount."

Nick had trouble taking that in. "The Ark still exists? You have it?"

"Yes."

"Where is it?"

"I want your word that you will not speak of what I am going to show you."

"I give you my word."

"Look to your left, Nick."

Nick turned to his left. A bank of lights came on, illuminating a raised dais covered with a blue cloth. Upon it, the true Ark of the Covenant shone golden under the bright lights. Seeing it, Nick realized the copy had been only a pale imitation. He took a deep breath. Something unseen emanated from the Ark, a sensation of radiant warmth that washed over him. A sense of subtle power. He wasn't a religious man, but he had an almost overwhelming urge to fall to his knees. He gazed on it for what seemed like a long time.

The lights went out. Nick turned back to the gallery. Something had just happened, with the sight of the Ark. Something important. He couldn't put his finger on what it was, exactly. Maybe it would become clear once there was time to think about it.

Adam's electronic voice echoed through the hangar. "Few have seen that," he said. "You have earned the privilege."

Nick knew what he had to do.

"I'll help you with Harker."

"We expected no less. If you wouldn't mind, please return to the car."

The driver waited by the open door. It was always the same man. Nick got in. The door closed and after a moment the Cadillac started and began to move. The ride back from wherever he'd been was silent. It seemed shorter, coming back.

The car stopped. Nick waited for the sound of the lock releasing. The drawer in the partition slid open. It contained his gun and phone. It also held a manila folder. The folder was stamped with red letters.

TOP SECRET
RESTRICTED CLEARANCE ONLY

The folder was scuffed, old. Adam's voice came through the speaker. "We debated giving this to you and decided that you had a need to know. The papers in that folder are the only copies. They will affect you personally. I suggest you think carefully before you do anything with what you find there."

Personally? What the hell did that mean?

The lock on the door clicked. Nick picked up his gun and phone. He took the folder. The drawer slid back into the partition.

"Goodbye, Nick."

He got out of the car and watched it pull away into the Washington traffic. It was early evening. He opened the folder. Inside was a sheaf of CIA surveillance and action reports. The first one was dated January, 1986.

He saw the name of the subject of the reports and knew things were about to change in ways he couldn't predict. *Joseph Edward Connor.*

Selena's father.

Then he saw the signature of the case officer handling the surveillance.

William Connor.

Selena's uncle.

251

Acknowledgements

My Wife, Gayle. Impossible, without her support.
Penny, Gloria, Bruce, Valerie. Thank you for your keen eyes and observations.
Another great cover from Neil Jackson. Thanks, Neil.

New Releases...

Be among the first to know when I have a new book coming out by subscribing to my newsletter. No spam or busy emails, only a brief announcement now and then. Just go to the link below. You can unsubscribe at any time...

http://alexlukeman.com/contact.html#newsletter

The Project Series

White Jade
The Lance
The Seventh Pillar
Black Harvest
The Tesla Secret
The Nostradamus File

Reviews by readers are welcome!